BOB FREVILLE

FILTHY MARAUDERS

©2022 by Bob Freville

All rights reserved.

First Edition Trade Paperback

ISBN: 9798423235987

Cover, layout and interior
K. Trap Jones

All persons in this book are fictitious, and any resemblance that may seem to exist to actual persons living or dead is purely coincidental. This is a work of fiction.

www.theevilcookie.com

ACKNOWLEDGMENTS

For Luke and for Eric, the kid who taught me how to be gross. I wish you were here, so I could make you nauseous.

AUTHOR'S NOTE

Did you ever wonder what it might look like if someone took the chicken fucking scene from John Waters' Pink Flamingos and stretched it out into an X-rated no holds barred bare-backed biker brawl? Of course you have. Don't try and lie to me. Oh, you're sick! You need help! Luckily, I got just the thing to cure your disease, Creep-o.

The Filthy Marauders is your fix, the story that's gonna quench your thirst for uncensored motorcycle maniacs, belly-shoving biker madness, and hug-the-bowl gross-outs so nasty you won't be able to look at your loved ones in the eyes without sobbing violently and dry-heaving.

The writing of The Filthy Marauders was intended as an exercise, to see if I could write a funny novelette in the days between the release of my political satire The Proud & the Dumb on December 12, 2021 and the first day of the new year. I'm proud (and probably dumb) to admit that I finished it in just under fifteen days and polished it over the holiday.

I gave myself a clear and simple writing prompt from the get: take the title of one of your favorite dirty blues songs and turn it into a splatterpunk story that pays homage to everything from The Glory Stompers and Born Losers to The Aristocrats and Night They Missed the Horror

Show. Somewhere along the way, I lost my ever-loving mind.

The end product is something that makes me smile, which is all a writer of any kind can really hope for.

"**We're** goin' down to Delacroix."

"How long?"

"Long as it takes to burn our bridges."

"Who's we?"

"Ten a the boys. Some prospects an' their old ladies."

"What for?"

"Fun in the sun," Spunk explained. "A quick run down the coast of Delacroix an' back. Whoop it up with the terminally sun-burned an' come back with a cash flow injection."

"Delacroix," the old buzzard repeated skeptically. "You'll be eatin' asphalt all the way there an' eatin' shit all the way back the Poles find out."

"We'll be a puff of smoke before those numb nuts swallow their first fly," Spunk assured him. "I'm bringing the Trog to be a spotter, provide cannon fodder if we need it. Nobody's rollin' up without us smellin' their stank a mile off."

The senior club member took a slow pull off a jar of moonshine, shaking his head, and staring daggers at the table in front of him.

"So, what do you want from me?" he asked.

"What do you think I want?" Spunk said. "We ain't the cocksuckin' Filthy Marauders without our chapter president."

"I'm not riding anymore, Spanky. Not after Squat Valley."

"Don't call me that, Nubs."

"Call ya what?"

"Spanky. It's misleading."

"It's your nickname, kid."

"Well, the guys call me 'Spunk.' On account a the amount a jizz -"

"Yeah, I got it," the president groaned, waving his callused hand at Spunk. "What do you want from me? You don't get to change your name, your name gets picked for ya. You're Spanky. On account a ya couldn't keep your hands off your pecker long enough to earn your cuts."

Spunk stiffened and his eyes went wild. The president could see it coming, so he wisely motioned to the chair opposite his desk.

"Calm down, brother. Take a seat if you need to. Remember who you're talkin' to."

"I earned my cuts," Spunk growled through gritted teeth the color of cave-aged cheddar. "I slaughtered your whole fam damnily and even chopped your kid up into little watermelon slices like you said. Took your daughter's cherry with a mangled nine-iron. Me and the boys even gave her a hole-in-one to show you we meaned business."

"Meant business," the chapter president corrected. "I know, you proved yourselves good. But that don't change the fact that you got your nickname already. You earn your cuts when the club decides you got the balls to hold it up. Your nickname's somethin' we choose to keep ourselves entertained, while you go about convincing us you're club material. We gotta do it that way cuz most of you dirty pigfuckers won't work out. You know all that."

"I do," Spunk said, hanging his head. "But I don't like to be called Spanky and you know it. This ain't no goddamn Our Gang, Chops."

Chops had been the president so long he'd

forgotten the hierarchy; the balls he was breaking belonged to his second-in-command. Chino "Spunk" Mahoney was a lot of things—a serial rapist, a necrophiliac, a bastard, and a stone cold killer. One thing he wasn't, however, was a punk. Despite being a perv who'd murdered his ma and forcibly sodomized his own pa, Spunk was what the club would call a stand-up guy. At least, their version of one.

As vice president of the club, Spunk had brought a surprisingly progressive flourish to the gang life; he started by holding a vote to install an actual female as the club's secretary, a position that had previously been held by a half-blind latch key kid with a trapper keeper, a wall calendar, and a box of Crayons; Spunk was also open about his mixed ethnicity and the fact that his deadbeat parents were unwed at the time of his conception, thus making it possible for people of different races and nationalities to be jumped into their fraternal ranks. The man was nuttier than a Chinese salad, but he was also the dude responsible for making the Filthy Marauders the first American biker gang to accept members of the Afro-Cuban, Honduran, Jamaican, and Gay communities, to name a few.

"It don't matter what you look like when you tan or whether you plug a lady or a man," Spunk used to say. "So long as you got a pair and you know how to use 'em, you're straight with the Filthy Marauders."

Chops thought about all this. He thought also of his own ironic nickname, "Chops," and how it had been lavished upon him because he couldn't grow mutton chops or, indeed, any kind of sideburns at a time when every man in America was rockin' a pair. For the last twelve years, he'd been lying to his younger brothers in the club, letting them believe the bogus legends that circulated, one that said he defeated an entire gang of rivals with a pair of well-seasoned pork chops. and the other a tall tale about karate chops and high kicks to the face of an eight-foot prison warden. Both of these stories were based on truth, but neither was steeped in the factual details of that truth. He decided a mea culpa was in order.

"Brother, I would gladly cut my hand for you if I thought the blood would quench your thirst for reprisal," he said.

"Some warm blood?" Spunk asked, sincerely meditating on the symbolic offer. "Mm..."

"You're absolutely right. It's a new dawn, a dawn you led us to. You the future a this damn thing. So, we should call you whatever you want to be called, Stunk."

"Spunk," the vice prez corrected.

"Thass what I said," Chops insisted. "Skunk."

Spunk shook his head and grit his teeth. "Alright, enough. You comin' or what?"

"What," Chops said.

"What do you mean?"

"I mean, 'Fuck no, I ain't goin!'"

"Why the shit not?"

"You blind as a got damn earthworm, boy? I ain't got no fuckin' legs!"

Spunk peered over the edge of the desk and took a fresh look at the grizzled pair of stumps that some asshole kid had given to their chapter president. The sight of the stumps always caused him to wince, which was strange—Chino Mahoney could take just about any sight of gore, goo, grundle, or ultra-violence, but the sight of his old buddy's amputated legs caused him to cringe and shudder. He believed the emotions brought to the surface by looking at his buddy's stumps were likely a reaction to the bitter irony surrounding them.

Chops didn't end up waddling around like Roscoe from Martin because of a bomb in a rice patty. He didn't even lose it to some chatted out fool from another gang. On the contrary, he had lost everything south of his sack by carelessly walking over a pile of lit fireworks at a neighborhood block party. Some twelve-year-old piss-pants kid had sneaked mortars into an otherwise harmless mix of blooming flowers and pyrotechnic stars. As the fuse sparked away into ash, Chops' blotto ass came storming through the block party looking to snatch some beers from a stranger's cooler, and the rest was history, the one he never shared with anyone. Anyone other than Spunk.

"Won't be the same without our older brother," Spunk said.

"Bring me back some booty."

"You know it," Spunk promised.

"And kid, don't forget to keep your eyes peeled for pyros... or Polacks."

Spunk held his ringed fingers aloft and fired off finger guns at the president.

"Fuckin' A."

Spunk hit the apex at the corner of Panorama and Valkyrie where the road opened up into six lanes and the land spread out to make room for the monolithic Otto Ranke Pharmaceutical Complex & Family Shopping Supercenter. As he straddled his V65 Magna, feeling the torque stirring his epididymis, ten cruddy, unwashed, and ragged motorheads appeared behind him on their bobbers and choppers. Some of them were wearing rusted yard sale brain buckets, others had nothing on their heads but the icy burn of the June air.

Moe the Mohel emerged from the throng and took his place by Spunk's side. Spunk smiled when he saw his oldest bud was riding with him.

"Fuck you lookin' at?" he joked.

"Bitch without a dick head when I'm done," Moe teased.

They called him The Mohel because he had a reputation for biting off the glans of his enemies. Moe had always been the modest type, but you didn't have to brag when you wore proof of your peccadilloes—a leather strap hung round Moe's neck, the low-hanging portion of the cord lined with shredded foreskin and severed cock helmets, each of them shriveled and hard, and yellowish-brown with age. Most of these trophies belonged to Charlie; Moe and his platoon were instructed to protect those who surrendered and aid in their resettlement, but the Mohel didn't like taking orders and he had his own designs in mind. Mostly they involved mouth-to-crotch penectomies and the re-purposing of the natives as lawn furniture.

Moe was a maniac, but he was also the only person Spunk truly trusted. There was a reason they called him the Wise One. He was the only dude they could count on to make preparations when one of their old ladies inevitably overdosed or fired on one of them and caught the wrong guy with the bullet. Moe used to own a florist shop... until it burned down quite by accident one hot summer night; he knew all about how to orchestrate a funeral, a wake, an internment, and, thanks to Sin City ordination-on-demand, a shotgun wedding. Moe was the epitome of a number two.

The boys hit a red light and decided to don some protection. As Spunk stared down his pal and began blipping the throttle, a station wagon full of square-ass cagers pulled up beside them, their car surrounded on all sides by the Filthy Marauders. Moe hooked a finger in their direction and smirked, as the gang reached into the leather panniers strapped to the sides of their machines, and removed large bottles of sunscreen. You can well imagine the look of horror, confusion and disgust on Dick and Jane's faces as this pack of grizzly, grimy gearheads placed big white bottles between their trembling thighs and squeezed, squirting themselves in their chests and chins with violent arcs of creamy white lotion. The bearded bastards spotted the squares' kids gaping at them, their doe-eyed faces plastered to the inside of the wagon's passenger side window. So they put on their best show, rubbing the cream into their oily, stubbled skin, and shaking their long hair about in mock-ecstasy.

Pa whacked his kids in their knees over the front seat, but this did not pry them away from the scene, nor did it stop Ma from following their sinewy arms with her eyes as they worked them this way and that, spreading out their fingers like monkeys to use up every last drop of the lotion.

"Looks like we got some Lookie-Lous," Moe said. "Whatcha wanna do?"

Spunk looked down at his buddy's makeshift necklace and reached out, snatching an old, blackened pickle tip off of the cord and chucking it through the crack in the square wife's window. The hairy canary head hit her in her lolling tongue, bouncing off and smacking the glass before landing like a spinning dreidel atop the squares' dashboard. Pa watched the hard dry cock head whirl around before drooping off the edge of the dash and landing in his console coffee. A hideous wail came from behind the station wagon's wheel as Mr. Cleaver lost his shit.

The Filthy Marauders whooped it up as the cager had a conniption. Moe slid the silver aviators down the bridge of his speckled nose and fixed Spunk with a stern look.

"That was straight cheatin,' Spunk."

"Call it recycling. You had your fun with it. Now, they get theirs. Keep up."

Spunk tore ass through the intersection and out onto Harridan Highway, trailed by Moe the Mohel and all their brothers and sisters.

Foxie Bonnie White had brought her ledger with her, to maintain the illusion that she was there for simple bookkeeping purposes, but everyone knew she wanted to get wet with the others. If there was one thing the Filipino broad with the big hair and long nails was good at besides answering phones and balancing a check book it was downing Irish car bombs and blowing shit up.

Spunk first met Foxie Bonnie when she was

working as a bookkeeper at some lard-ass Frenchman's strip club, a place called La Chatte in Quebec's Red-Light District. The owner, Bastien, owed them their due and hadn't paid in months. They'd already sent prospects to break three of his hairy sausage fingers, but the fractures and beatings seemed not to faze him. So, Spunk and Moe had showed up in their official capacity as club representatives to flay the fat frog, but when they got there the place was overrun by lusty sailors and drunken skels. A pair of French fuck bois were grabbing Foxie's ass as she crossed the bar with ledger in hand.

When Spunk and Moe started destroying the dudes that were hassling her, Foxie Bonnie went ape. The ballistic bitch nailed them in the groin with a pool cue and started shouting about how she didn't need no man to protect her. Spunk's attempts to calm her ass down only led to more bloodshed as her Filipino blood flared up and she started breaking bottles, spitting blood and broken glass in their eyes. When the crowd dispersed, they were left standing in a semi-circle on the barroom floor, matted from head to toe in each others' blood and hair as Debby Boone crooned "You Light Up My Life" on the club's P.A. To this day, the gang couldn't hear that song without laughing their heads off.

Foxie had convinced them all she was coming on the Delacroix run to keep an eye on their expenditures, but in her heart she knew she was really there to keep an eye on the one they called Brainiac. Homegirl had a jones for the weirdo's jock and the jones was so strong, she'd gone out and got herself a broke ass sled of her own, just so she could make the run with the rest of them.

Foxie Bonnie White wasn't the only female

making the run. A couple of the new guys had brought their old ladies, but they hadn't yet learned what Filthy Marauders do to prospect pussy. This was another reason Foxie Bonnie had rationalized her presence: she knew how to keep the MC in line when the wheels started coming off and, if given an option, most of the prospects' old ladies would choose cunnilingus with a Filipino secretary over deep-throating some fat, old organ donor.

Despite her presence, the run was still a glorified sausage fest.

There was Scalps, the club's sergeant at arms, so nicknamed because he wore his victims' scalped hair after he went prematurely bald at the age of seventeen. Scalps was the herbal specialist and resident wook, but he was good with a knife and better with a bong.

Then you had Bones, the club's rail-thin money man, who served as treasurer under Foxie. Bones made up for the lack of meat on him by protecting everybody's bread; when the gang made its bi-annual Poker Run, it was Bones who saw fit to pickpocket their wallets once they'd gone on a drinking binge. In short, he was the guy everyone went to when it was time to file their taxes.

After the treasurer there was Brainiac, the club's Road Captain, a scary quiet young man who joined their ranks by simply being disgusting without effort. Brainiac was the smartest, calmest, most collected homey anyone could have at their back, but the dude was straight gross. All they had ever seen him in was the suit on his back, form-fitting funereal black threads that tapered down into coattails, with a white V-neck underneath and a black Western-style bow tie looped about his scraggly neck. Brainiac actually wore his cuts over the suit jacket, which looked about as strange as any article of clothing could look. And Brainiac wasn't just odd in garb, he was odd in general. The boy quoted Epicurus, Kierkegaard, and Kant as casually as he cut a fart.

The gang first met Brainiac at a roadside food truck where they'd been running a train on a self-proclaimed "hot dog hooker." As they finished all over the inside of her work station, Brainiac called out from his perch on an adjacent park bench. The gang heard a sharp whistle and peered out to see what was up. Their eyes met a gaunt little man in an antique suit, legs crossed and a napkin draped across his lap, reading from a copy of de Sade's Justine, and absently squirting an entire bottle of hot mustard on a single sardine.

"You got a problem, Ace?" one of them had asked.

"Not as such," Brainiac said. "I will confess to a craving however. If y'all would be so kind as to mop up your mess and bring it out on a generous slab of raw meat, I would be forever in your debt."

There was a long, stunned silence, as they all looked at each other, at a loss for how best to respond.

"Any of you mongos ever heard of steak tartare?" he asked rhetorically. "I take mine with a good dollop of man-made aioli."

They were so aghast that they followed his every instruction.

"And don't hesitate to give it a good stink fingering," he added. "I like it dirty, but I also like it tender."

He licked the tip of his finger and carefully turned to the next page of Justine before digging deeply into his nostril and dragging out an aperitif. Most impressively, he never broke his concentration on the book and would later recount every word of it to them as they gleefully jumped him into their club.

Ever since, Brainiac had been the mind behind the guys, a filthy gentleman among filthy savages who could wield a shank as swiftly as he could dispense with a witty barb. If there were logistics to talk through, he was your guy, and so long as Brainiac was around, you didn't need the weather channel because he studied meteorological activity like it was his job.

Then you got Gary and the other twerps bringing up the back. Gary was your typical meathead with the potential to become a patchmember if he played his cards right. The problem was, no one could get a fix on the dude. They figured he only stuck around to stare at Foxie Bonnie White because it was all he ever did when the rest of the club was busy boning and breaking shit. Gary had been a hangaround for three years until they finally told him he was a prospect out of sheer exasperation; they knew he wasn't going anywhere and it didn't make sense for him to continue loitering on the side lines like the village idiot if he was going to be privy to any of their meets. What disturbed Spunk and the fellas was Gary's lack of ambition. He didn't seem hungry enough to reach for his cuts.

The thing that kept him in their good graces was his weed (the dude could grow a hybrid that would knock your stones out of your eye sockets) and the fading image of him out-grossing the Mohel at a chain restaurant.

The Filthy Marauders had been whooping it up at Juicy Lucy's, the East coast's X-rated answer to Hooters, when the little piss ant sidled up like he was the Tazmanian Devil and decided to do his thing. Moe the Mohel had taken a dare from the other guys in the club. The portly perv hopped up on a table where a Jesus freak couple was seated and shouted, "I'll show y'all how to do some Christian mingling!" Then he took down his funky black leather pants and proceeded to void his bowels all over their booth. All the while the rest of the gang howled like bitches in heat and slammed their shot glasses down on the bar. Suddenly, Gary walks over, all of five foot nothing, with Flock of Seagulls bangs, and stares the Mohel down.

Moe jumped off the fish kids' table top and faced the little prick with his typically mean mug on, daring him to make a move.

"If you feelin' froggy, take your best shot," he said.

So, Gary did just that, picking up the massive mud pie Moe had left on the randos' table and stuffing it in his face without breaking his gaze. After chewing and swallowing, he bent over the table, as if inspecting it. Then he did the unexpected: the little shaver cupped his hand and scooped up Moe's scattered gravy spray, slurping it down with a straw before picking a piece of corn from his teeth and flicking it at Moe's cuts.

Moe stood there in shock for a beat, then wailed with laughter, and slapped the kid on the back. Gary knew he was golden when the old berserker turned to the nearest server, wrested a bottle of tequila from their grip, and handed it off to him, urging the ballsy twerp to drain it.

He might have seemed dense and inadequately motivated, but Gary had the club's trust. When one of their bikes wouldn't turn over, he'd give up his own machine to get them where they were going. If they were on their way to shake someone down and they felt the heat on them, Gary would volunteer to create a diversion, usually one that landed him in jail. Then there was the matter of their steady girls, thirsty bitches who could be every bit as jealous as their straight homemaking counterparts. When Spunk knocked up some cheap piece of ass at the Star Bright Lounge and the fuck hole started calling his pad at all hours, Gary assured Spunk's old lady that it was all a lie.

"That gash is psycho," Gary told her. "I threw her a bone at a club barbecue and now she wants it four times a day. When I don't give her my leg, she goes off accusing people of shit. If that slore is preggers, she's preggers with my seed."

Satisfied that Spunk's old lady was relieved, Gary took his bike across town to the Meat Packing District and parked behind a shuttered butcher's shop. Then he hoofed it across the lot and over a fence to where the piece of ass laid her head at night. He waited until the lights had gone out in the other units of the building and then he knocked softly on her apartment door.

When the piece of ass answered, Gary was ready for her with a fresh shave and a stethoscope. She looked him up and down, noting the black leather satchel gripped in his clean white hands and the gleaming stethoscope around his smooth young neck. He looked like he could have been a med student, which is what he was counting on. And he looked her up and down, noting the swollen ankles and the slight bump beneath her halter top. This was all the confirmation he needed.

"Pardon the intrusion," he told her.

"What's this about?" she asked. "It's late."

"The club sent me," Gary promised. "They thought I should check up on you. Make sure the child's alright."

"I guess that'd be okay," she said, removing the thin metal chain from the door.

Gary entered the cramped apartment and looked around suspiciously.

"What did you say your name was?"

"I didn't," Gary intoned. "I told you, the club sent me."

"What club?"

"You know what club," he insisted.

"Did Spunk send you or what?"

"Thass right," Gary said.

He slapped her in the forehead with the back of his hand, causing her to lose her footing.

"Oh, you feel feverish, ma'am."

Gary reached around with his free hand, cupping his rough palm around the small of her back.

"We'll need to give you something for that. STAT."

Gary came up with a syringe and the piece of ass's eyes bulged.

"Standard practice," he assured her. "It's just a mild sedative with analgesic to get that fever down."

Before the gash could process this, her focus was gone, as were her motor skills. Gary laid her out like a dress on a card table in her kitchen nook. She didn't put up a fight. Couldn't. One slender hand went passively to her belly, but Gary brushed it away as he reached into the black leather bag. He pulled out a portable aspirator and set it down on the table beside her. Her head fell lazily to the side and she squinted at the device that was just out of focus.

"What's that?" she asked.

"That's, uh... that's our baby portable... sonogram," Gary lied. "That's how we see if this kid's gone bad like his dad."

"Bad?" she asked.

"Yep."

Gary attached a tube to the aspirator, then affixed a cannula to the other end. Then he strapped on two rubber gloves and ran his covered fingers over the girl's swollen gut, feeling around for the precise location of Spunk's bastard seed.

"Looks like there might be a slight problem," he said.

"What?" she groaned drowsily. "What that mean?"

"Means we're gonna have to take a closer look is all."

Gary lifted the long plain skirt the piece of ass wore on her way home from her titty bar night shift. He stuck four fingers inside her and she groaned again.

"You're doin' great," he said. "Now, you'll just feel a little more pressure."

"What?"

The loyal little twerp took firm grip of her right flank and rammed the cannula deep into her dry twat, then he reached over and flipped a switch on the aspirator. It jumped to life with an electric hum and the sucking noise began. With his right hand, he turned a knob up as far as it would go, leading the strung out slore to yowl as the machine suctioned up every small, slippery, amorphous particle of Spunk's mistake. When he turned the machine off a few minutes later, the cannula had sucked up some of the stripper's insides with it, prompting the club to christen the aspirator the Gash Masher 3000.

The next morning, the kid arrived at the clubhouse bright-eyed and bushy-tailed. He walked up to Spunk with a package in each fist.

"Pick a hand," he said.

"Right," Spunk guessed.

Gary opened his right palm and dropped a Zip

Loc full of malformed fetal appendages into Spunk's open palms.

"This is it?" Spunk asked. "Looks smaller'n I imagined."

"Yep," Gary said.

"What's in the other hand?"

Gary flung the other package in the air and Spunk caught it. The cardboard seal at the top of the bag read, "Grow Amazing Live SEA-MONKEYS. It's the LIVING TRUTH!"

"What's this?"

"Next time you wanna get your dick wet without a jimmy, just add water," Gary said, swaggering away.

***

The trip down was always a stone bummer. Once your nether regions went numb from the steady rumble, the brain got lazy and every mile became a fight to drown out the call of the void. After hours on the bike with countless street signs in your rear view, the urge to go over the side and play Tag with a tractor trailer grew almost inevitable.

To keep themselves straight, the Filthy Marauders would have to ingest a lot of chemicals. This is where Scalps was clutch. He could maintain a straight line using his ankles on the handlebars, while he handed out balloons of sneeze and fresh peyote buttons to every rider around him. By the time they left their home turf, the whole gang was typically lit and disturbing pedestrian drivers with their loud recital of the dirty blues.

"Makes no difference, baby, where you go! I got somethin' I want you to know! I got ants in my pants, baby, for you," they'd holler as Bo Carter blared from Spunk's mounted motorcycle radio speakers.

This is when the drool would dangle off their stupid faces like a dog's ears drooping out a window and, eventually, detach itself as they picked up speed. The trip to Delacroix was different. The men were uncharacteristically somber and many of them had a bad feeling from the start.

Spunk didn't let it stop him from keeping morale up. As they idled at stop lights, he'd set his boots down on either side of the Magna and say, "You boys hear the one about the crusty ole biker out on a ride in the country? Dude pulls up to a tavern in the middle of nowhere and decides to head in for a couple shots. As he heads in, he sees a sign advertisin' two dollar beers, three dollar cheeseburgers, and fifty dollar handjobs. So, he takes out his wallet, looks inside, and thinks about it for a second. Satisfied he's got what he needs, my man heads over to the bartender, some pretty little coos in a sun dress. The ole biker gives her a wave and the coos says, 'How can I help ya?' The ole biker says, 'Ma'am, you the one givin' the handjobs?' She looks at 'em and says, 'Why, yes. That'd be me.' So, he leans into her ear and whispers, 'Well, you wash your hands real good now, lil lady, cuz this motherfucker wants himself a cheeseburger.'"

The laughs continued as they headed south. Along the way, Moe spotted a half-naked Rabbi on the side of the highway. The old Jewish scholar's pants were off and his penis was mutilated. He was holding a sign, which read, "No More Tips. Turn Back Now." He wasn't entirely convinced it was a hallucination, so he ate some more peyote buttons, and tried to focus on the radio. Blind Boy Fuller was moaning the verses to "Worn Out Engine

Blues."

***

The Filthy Marauders arrived in Delacroix at around five in the evening, just as the sun suffered its nightly case of whiskey dick. The wide open sky was poon tang pink as the firmaments cleared. Great swatches of fire red hinted at a storm that had just passed or might soon arrive. It was too late in the day for them to compete in the official tournaments at the Annual Hilljack Games, but as any resident of Durr City could have told you, hilljack games weren't technically over until every tourist had left Delacroix County penniless. In the meantime, there would be plenty of seeds to spit, armpits to serenade, and toilet seats to hurl at strangers. It wasn't June in Delacroix without hubcaps on heads, hornet's nests on groins, or beer guts in mud pits.

When the gang reached the town square, they were shocked to find the gazebo area empty. At this time of the day, the place was usually popping with toothless perverts of every stripe, most of 'em slamdancing to Cock Rock by the gazebo, grabbing gobfuls of barbecue off strangers' plates, or free-balling it out second-story windows, and landing on passing cars. But that night none of that was happening. Instead, the gazebo was bereft of any sign of life and the street was free of congestion.

"Somethin' smells like my ex-wife's box," said Scalps.

"Fishier than a fresh diaper in the Hudson River," Bones agreed.

Spunk scanned their surroundings, one hand on his bike, and the other on his Bowie knife.

"What do ya say, Brain?"

Brainiac regarded the E.M. Cioran paperback in his lap and read from the page.

"'If we could see ourselves as others see us, we would vanish on the spot.'"

"Profound," Bones said sarcastically. "Why don't you go eat an abortion or something, Cioran."

"Mmm," Brainiac mocked. "Don't tease me, I'm starving."

"So?" Spunk snapped. "Are we in consensus?"

"I say we fuck off before we get pinched," Scalps suggested.

"Yeah," Bones agreed. "I'm getting lightheaded."

"Did you prick your finger?" Brainiac asked, already knowing full well that he hadn't.

Bones removed a small testing kit from his side bag and began checking his blood glucose level.

"Shit," he finally said.

Brainiac tossed him a Snickers.

"Well, gents, shall we split like a cheerleader on prom night?"

"Nah," Spunk said.

"What?" Scalps asked. "The fuck, Spunk?"

"Kill your engines," Spunk instructed, scanning the area through squinted eyes.

Scalps looked at him skeptically, as did the other club members, who exchanged smirks like their older brother was dense. Brainiac knew better than to challenge the status quo, unless he had something particularly witty lined up. He killed his engine and the new recruits followed suit. Scalps and the boys did so begrudgingly. Gary looked to Foxie Bonnie White, for whom he felt a familial protectiveness. He knew the bitch could fight like a man, but he also knew knives cut deeper than press-on nails, and he wasn't about to watch her end up like his biological sister, face cut clean down the middle by some cholo outside a chicken shack. He curled his fingers around a Smith & Wesson Special Ops blade in his pocket and nodded to Foxie Bonnie. Together they killed the lights of their respective machines.

"If you think going silent is smart, consider what we actually done," Scalps said.

"What?" Spunk whispered.

"We just gone blind and black in the pitch darkness. Might as well string ourselves up and tell someone to kick us in the ass."

"Shut up," Spunk demanded.

A faint rustling drew his attention. Somewhere on the opposite side of the street, a tinkering came. It was as intermittent as a clock with faulty batteries, but it was unmistakable. After listening for a few moments, Spunk reached for the knife on his belt.

"Whatcha gonna do?" Scalps said. "Slice up the night?"

"Shut your rape hole, Baldy."

That's when another tinkering echoed out, this one from their right, somewhere beyond the Durr River dock. It competed with the flapping of boat covers in the cold night breeze, building a soundscape that was unnerving in its familiarity. When a clang issued from the direction they'd come from, the Filthy Marauders knew they were good and well fucked. The only place to go was into the murky, gelid water of the Durr River below dock.

"Cock," Spunk exclaimed.

Moe tongued his lips on instinct.

"Get cocked," Spunk demanded. "All you motherfuckers."

The Marauders did as they were told, pulling the cocks of their guns back against the tension of their springs, some of the younger men using two hands to accomplish this, others reaching around for keys or knives or lengths of chain in lieu of firearms.

"We go together on the third P."

"The third P?" Gary said, frowning.

"You shall see," Brainiac whispered. "You shall see, baby G."

The tinkering came again, replaced at once by the eerie silence of the cold marina.

"Ready?" Spunk asked.

Moe swallowed hard. "Ready."

"Ready," Scalps said, pulling a live grenade from the deep cavern of his belly button. He brought the explosive to his face, plunging the striker lever with his thumb and yanking the pin free with his teeth.

"Ready?" Spunk repeated.

"As always, my good man," Brainiac promised, holding a jar of moonshine and a lighter in his free hand.

"Pay dirt," Spunk said.

The tinkering came again. The boys shifted into neutral, easing off the clutch as if it were the throat of a thieving whore.

"Pussy," Spunk said.

The tinkering came louder and more erratic. The Marauders steeled themselves, gloved hands squeezing the clutch like a pair of juicy titties, choking and releasing them to feed the throttle.

In the black void surrounding them they could suddenly see silver shafts of steel, silver metallic weapons sure to be leveled against them. They braced themselves and engaged the clutch.

"Power!" Spunk hollered.

The Marauders burned out, wheels sending up clouds as massive and gray as the heads of ancient dragons. A croaking growl of V-twin engines mingled with the tit-ripping bomb of wide-open throttles. Mufflers sparked and flamed, and the balls of the young Marauders bounced to life as they broke into packs of three and headed into uncertain oblivion. As they readied their whips and Colts and Smith & Wesson M & Ps, Spunk saw a figure emerge from the darkness, with what looked like a sword buried in his crotch. Thinking the man injured, Spunk called off the dogs.

"Two finger taco!" he shouted over the din of their bikes.

The boys did as they were told, curling two fingers around the front brakes and applying pressure like they were finger-banging a bunch of chrome plated virgins. As their bikes gradually slowed and they came to rock back and forth, the Cunty Scoundrels stepped out of the abyss. Each of the Scoundrels had a long, thin cylindrical rod protruding from his meatus, and each of the rods clinked into the steel toes of the Scoundrels' Tallahassee western shit-kickers—the source of all the tinkering. Spunk got off his bike and started over to the obvious leader, a stout gender-nonspecific individual with a flaming bouffant hairdo, six thick stainless steel nipple piercings, and the word "TWAT" scrawled across their chest in reddish-brown dung. They wore a torn-and-tattered night gown with the chest cut out.

Spunk cocked his Browning High Power and held it aloft for the leader to see. "What the fuck you want, Twat?"

"I much prefer Cunt, Spunky."

That's when the leader seized Spunk by his wrist and eased the barrel of the Browning handgun deep into the chasm of their throat, cleaning the smooth bore inside with circles of their serpentine tongue, and working it up and down until they moaned gutturally and smiled broadly. Spunk was astonished to see a round from his own handgun sticking out from between the leader's clenched teeth.

The leader shut their mouth and the bullet disappeared. They swallowed with a hard gulp and sighed a satisfied sigh, beaming beatifically at Spunk. The Cunty Scoundrels whistled in delight, while the Filthy Marauders maintained their guard.

"A gentleman never spits," the crazy twat said.

"Who are you freaks?" Spunk asked.

"It's me, Spunk. Uncle Cousin Debbie!"

"Uncle Cousin Debbie?"

"As sure as I eat shit," Uncle Cousin Debbie declared.

"Never seen ya before."

"Of course ya has," Uncle Cousin Debbie insisted. "We hooked up at last year's Hilljack Games right here in Durr!"

"We wasn't here for last year's games," Scalps chimed in.

"Sure ya was," one of the Scoundrels insisted, waving his mechanically-enhanced wang in Moe the Mohel's face. Moe slurped his glans hesitantly but curiously.

"Yeah, I'd remember this schnozzle," Moe said. "We don't know you cunts from a glory hole in Guyana."

"Well, sure ya do," Uncle Cousin Debbie insisted. "You..."

Uncle Cousin Debbie rolled their tongue around in their mouth, struggling with something caught in their gums. They reached into their pocket and produced a toothpick.

"Pardon me, I've got some dick in my teeth."

Spunk craned his neck to look at his fellow Marauders in disbelief as Uncle Cousin Debbie dug at their gums with the wooden pick. Finally, they spit blood and grinned.

"Of course you was here," they insisted.

"Hell no," Scalps said. "My old lady had a case of the piles. Bitch had to keep my ass home to manage the clusters."

"We were here," Brainiac confirmed. "You brought your ass cluster with you."

"Thass right," Uncle Cousin Debbie said. "We all took turns popping them 'rhoids into our eyes and mouths. The candy apple steamer challenge, as I recall."

"You expect me to believe we met people we don't remember at an event we don't remember goin' to?"

"I remember," Brainiac said.

"Can it!" Spunk demanded.

"It's the got damn Summer Hilljack Tournaments," a seven-foot tall cross-dressing bodybuilder explained as he ran a finger down Bones' bony chest.

"And you are?"

"Prettypony Piper," the cross-dressing gargantuan said. "Useta be Pipecock Jackson, but then that Scratch Perry dude bit my style."

"What's that y'all got stickin' outta your glans?" Spunk asked.

"It's called sounding," Uncle Cousin Debbie said. "We're getting a jump on training for next year's genital endurance challenge."

"So, what do you want from us?"

"Ain't it obvious, Spunk?"

Spunk shook his head. Uncle Cousin Debbie smiled broadly, exposing teeth coated in crystal meth and cum.

"We wanna party like we did last year."

"You sayin' you want to party to the point we

don't remember who in the fuck filled all our holes last night?"

"Ya damn skippy!"

"You're sayin' you want to party with us until we suffer short-term memory loss and experience temporary blindness?"

"Yup!"

Spunk looked around at the Cunty Scoundrels, some of them in cock rings, others wearing surgical studs, and all of them brandishing bottles of booze and bundles of elicit substances instead of weapons.

"Well, awright then!"

***

The Cunty Scoundrels had taken the Filthy Marauders to the far end of the marina where a party boat had been erected on a large wooden square. It was the sort of thing you would expect to see in a bad shark movie, but the boys didn't seem to mind. As it rocked back and forth, casting shadows from the colorful paper lanterns over their heads, the two gangs held their bottles high and moaned along to the lyrics of "Freakin' at the Freaker's Ball" by Dr. Hook.

"'White ones, black ones, yellow ones, red ones. Necrophiliacs lookin' for dead ones. The greatest of the sadists and the masochists too. Screaming please hit me and I'll hit you.'"

The filthy cunts and the marauding scoundrels shared a mad laugh as they sang. Then Brainiac pulled a Luger on Steven, a rather burly member of the Cunty Scoundrels, as he commenced grinding up and down the length of Brainiac's right flank.

"You'll have to forgive Steven," Uncle Cousin Debbie said. "He's a frotteurist."

"A what now?" Spunk said.

Brainiac returned the Luger to its holster and licked his fingers, turning the page on an issue of Popular Mechanics. "Carry on."

"Thank you," Steven purred, grinding more vigorously as Brainiac returned to an article on thermodynamics.

"He's into frotteurism," Uncle Cousin Debbie explained. "Boy's turned on by rubbing himself on strangers."

"There's a perv for every joint a the human body, iddn't there?" Spunk mused.

"You damn right," Uncle Cousin Debbie agreed. "So, y'all gonna be in town for a minute?"

"Yeah, why?"

"Nah... just seems odd is all. You showin' up after most of the real anarchy's already passed."

"Whatchoo mean?" Spunk snapped. "We made it in time for tomorrow's toilet bowl toss, didn't we?"

"Yeah," Debbie agreed. "But the lumberjackin's already over. Y'all didn't come all the way out here just to use some toilet seats as boomerangs, didja?"

"What is this?" Spunk asked. "I thought we was havin' a soiree, not talkin' business."

"Why? You got business here?"

Spunk shook his head and grinned.

"You're a real card, ain'tcha, Uncle Cousin?"

"Debbie," Uncle Cousin Debbie insisted.

"Debbie."

"Delacroix's a janky place, my friend. I like to keep an eye on my friends is all."

"Well, cheers to that."

Spunk took a thirsty swig off a quart of Rusty Lung, letting the suffocating taste of malt and molasses wash over his taste buds before chasing it with the vapors from a fat blunt.

Debbie regarded the half-empty bottle with

concern.

"Better choke off the neck a that Rusty Lung, pirate."

"Why's that?"

"Cuz we didn't even get freaky yet."

Spunk laughed and handed the bottle off to Uncle Cousin Debbie, who took it and drained it in one gulp, breathing fire.

"Well, suck me silly," Spunk exclaimed. "I won't stop ya."

Uncle Cousin Debbie motioned for three strippers to come over from a corner of the party float. As soon as Spunk saw them, he regretted it. These strippers were too jacked up even for him.

"Uh, look," he said, holding a hand up in Debbie's chest.

"Wuzzat?" they asked.

"We appreciate all ya hospitality, Uncle Cousin Debbie, but ... I ain't nearly inebriated enough to look at them heffers, much less mount one of 'em."

"Oh honey," Uncle Cousin Debbie exclaimed, feigning upheaval and tickling Spunk in the face with a frilly handkerchief. "You flatlanders are terribly judgmental. Don't y'all know that it's what's inside that counts?"

"Well..."

"And lemme tell you, boy... you gonna like they insides, one way or the other. One with the eye is Laverne. You can brain that gal with your bone or a stone. Either way, ain't nobody gonna miss her. Certainly not her social security case worker."

"What about the Lady Lump?" Spunk said, grimacing in the direction of another skank in a black string bikini, her pregnant belly spilling over her black bottoms. "Looks like she knows how to fill those unders."

"Thass Hildie," Debbie said. "Five bucks gets

your dick brown. Throw in a stem and she'll let ya talk dirty to her unborn."

"I think I'll pass," Spunk said. "This weekend's all about the boys."

"Thass what I like to hear," Uncle Cousin Debbie said. "Someone gettin' promoted or is someone poppin' they cherry?"

"Both. Thinkin' 'bout giving Gary his cuts."

"Which one's Gary?" Debbie asked.

"The dumb shit salivating over my secretary."

At the far end of the party float, Gary stood uncomfortably close to Foxie Bonnie White, licking, shooting, and sucking shots of El Jimador Silver.

"Mazel tov," Uncle Cousin Debbie cheered.

"So," Spunk said. "Why the rods in your ... rods?"

"I told ya," Uncle Cousin said. "We training, boy! That and it's the future of kink. When we finally vault over that bar at the Hilljack Games, we will experience a Tantric internal orgasm the likes of which no man or woman has ever experienced. It will be like our chakras have ejaculated into our cores."

"You could always save yourself the trouble and split a Toblerone," Spunk reasoned. "Very decadent."

The pair moon-walked over to their respective men as Wynonie Harris sang "Keep On Churnin' Till The Butter Comes." Thus began the funky, freaky festivities. Steven massaged Brainiac to completion with the top of his bald pate. Scalps and Moe took turns working out on two twins, both named Little John, each of them wearing a matching purple codpiece. And sooner or later, the whole gang of scoundrels had spermed in each others' eye sockets, sucking out the resulting seed with straws and spitting it in the air. This created a perfect seasonal shower, which landed gently over their bodies as they undulated and bruised each other, beating, drinking, and fucking their way into a temporary coma. Scalps removed the hair piece he'd taken off the skull of a gas station attendant on their way down to Delacroix, revealing the infected stitches he'd sewn into the top of his own head with a hook and some fishing line.

"What do these remind ya of?" he asked his new friends.

"Your old lady's anal speed bumps," Uncle Cousin Debbie shouted with glee.

Soon, the uncle cousin was down on bent knee. They pressed their fingers together and squeezed, opening wide as each yellow bilious pustule burst like a grape over their tongue.

This was the last thing any of them would remember. Later, Brainiac would swear up and down that his last memory was of Uncle Cousin Debbie riding Spunk's 'stache, and Spunk would agree, because he really wasn't in a position to dispute anything. The butter had been churned.

FLIM-FLAMMED & FUCKED OVER

The last thing the vice president of the Filthy Marauders could picture was Uncle Cousin Debbie, their nightgown torn straight down the middle, bulbous cock helmet flopping this way and that, and their big gray balls bouncing up and down on a hobby horse. And the last words Uncle Cousin Debbie uttered still rang out in his ears: "Ya ever heard a bath salts?"

The taste of dried blood on his tongue told him he'd heard of 'em now and the bits of brain he dislodged from between his teeth confirmed as much.

"Must have been a whale of a time," he said to himself.

His eyes stung like he'd spent all night pouring hot sauce in them. The others were even worse for wear.

If their memories were hazy, their first sight most certainly was not. The Filthy Marauders awoke in a boathouse to faces full of feathers. The prospects were the first to go. They made a mad dash for the bay doors and found themselves a pile of human sushi rolls on the slick metal floor. It was clear they weren't supposed to leave.

Spunk's clothes were all but completely missing, but his watch was still on his wrist. He checked the time.

"We're late for the meet."

A laugh came from his feet. Spunk looked down

and found Moe sitting criss-cross apple sauce on the cold metal floor, a flaming cigarette butt between his lips.

"No, we ain't, brutha."

"What do ya mean? We're fuckin' late to meet the cat with the coordinates to the stash."

Spunk called out to the others, some of whom were still unconscious on the hard metal floor. "Spectacles, testicles, wallets, and watch, boys!"

"We're right on time, Spunk."

"What the fuck do you mean?"

"Stash we was supposed to raid. What did ya say your contact's name was?"

"I don't know, Joe Some-Shit, said he met us on our last run. Knows the Poles, wants to get us square."

"Jesus Christ," Moe said, shaking his head.

"What?"

"Why didn't ya just hand him the fucking gun, El Presidente?"

"What is this shit?" Scalps asked. "Are you disrespecting our VP?"

Moe waved a hand in Scalps' face.

"Calm down, Toupee. Don't get in my way."

"What the fuck are you saying to me?" Spunk asked. "Dude said he knew us. We did belly shots with 'em. Said he useta live down the coast. Said he porked your sister if I'm bein' honest."

"And this dude who you don't know, but he knows you, says he gonna send you where for this stash?"

"A boathouse off the coast. Why?"

Moe gestured to their surroundings, a steel and aluminum structure with impossibly high ceilings and what appeared to be sound-proofed walls. In the corners of the room stood stacks of wooden pallets, boat motors, and dense steel drums. The place smelled like ammonia and death. Spunk surveyed the room apprehensively.

"Suck my cysts," he intoned in defeat.

He looked to the bay where their fallen prospects rested in pieces about as thick as New York strip steaks, their blood swirling down a jerry rigged drain in the floor.

"Brothers, ya got your wallets?"

"Yeah," they all groaned in unison.

Spunk looked over and saw Bones sitting atop a bloody old boat cooler, oversize chocolate bar in hand. A mess of liquid milk chocolate encircled his crusty mouth as he chewed.

"They rolled us and took our cuts, but they let Bones keep his chocolate bar." Spunk laughed. "Ain't that some shit?"

"Got damn," Moe said, grimacing at Bones' smeared mouth. "We oughtta call ya ass Analingus the way you walkin' around with that shit all over ya mouth."

Bones stared his biker brother down as he continued to chew. Moe laughed.

"Ya got ya weapons?" Spunk asked.

Each of them checked and to their amazement, their chains, whips, and knives remained.

"Affirmative," Gary called out.

"Yep," the others muttered.

Spunk surveyed the boathouse interior warily.

"Something's foul.".

"Way to state the got damn obvious," Moe barked.

"Give him a break," Scalps growled. "Before I break you."

"Don't hurl threats, Mr. Clean. I'll bite ya cock off and spit it in ya momma's cunt."

"Goddammit, Moe. You know I ain't never met my maw."

Scalps' chin started quivering with emotion. Spunk threw an arm around him, consoling him gently, while mean mugging Moe.

"Ya always take it just a bit too far, don't ya, ya Hebe?"

"Don't 'Hebe' me. I married a Jew, that don't make me any less of a brutha."

"How ya gonna make fun a the simpleton?"

"Huh?" Scalps said, looking up from where his face rested against Spunk's arm pit.

"You know my man's herbal escapades left his ass flame-broiled."

"Ain't my fault Scalps flipped his lid on some vision quest."

"Vision quest?" Scalps said.

"Apologize to your brother," Spunk demanded.

Moe hung his head.

"We really need to do this shit right now?"

Spunk stared Moe down with resolve.

"Sorry, Scalps," Moe sighed. "No disrespect, man. But if ya keep talkin' smack, I'ma saw ya pecker off with a piece of paper, fold it up like origami, and stuff it in ya dead grandma's cooch."

For whatever reason, this drew laughter from the teary-eyed Scalps. He crossed to Moe and they hugged it out.

"Alright," Spunk said, hitting each of them in the crotch with his knuckles. "Sac up. We gotta figure this out."

"You say it as if common sense doesn't completely elude you lot," Brainiac said.

Spunk shot the Brain a dirty look. "If ya ain't got nothin' nice to say, Brainiac."

"What?" Brainiac challenged.

"Shut ya stank ass trap before I fill it with milt," Moe snapped, scanning the room for clues to its design.

"Promises, promises," Brainiac said, staring down at his fingernails.

"There's a grid," Moe told no one in particular. "The floor. It's a grid pattern, like it's designed to open up into smaller segments."

A clapping sound came from above, the sort of slow clap that Americans associate with an underdog's triumph. It was Uncle Cousin Debbie, but they weren't clapping. Clapping never got this sticky.

***

Uncle Cousin Debbie beat one off into a Big Gush from 9-Eleven.

"Uncle Cousin Debbie!" Spunk exclaimed.

"The two and only," Debbie declared, pretending to bow as they stirred their slurry with a colored twisty straw. "Y'all looked so lonely down there."

Uncle Cousin Debbie gave the Big Gush one last stir and then knocked it back, draining the slushie's splooge-filled contents.

Moe cringed. "Oh, you nasty, girl!"

"Rich," Debbie said. "comin' from a man who bites off dick heads like they broccoli florets."

"You don't see me bitin' off my own," Moe reasoned.

"Enough!" Spunk shouted. "What the fuck's goin' on, Cuzz?"

"Uncle Cuzz," Debbie corrected.

"Uncle Cuzz. What in the Devil's dirty draws is this shit all about?"

"It's simple, Spunk." Uncle Cousin Debbie held out a fat cigar for lighting.

A slender, freckled hand reached out with a Zippo and lit Debbie's cigar. The hand belonged to a man with enough blond arm hair to play Madonna in a made-for-TV movie. There was only one man it could be ... Bartek, the lesser of two Poles.

"Ah, fuck," Spunk murmured. "The Poznanski Brothers? Bartek, Borys. What's happenin,' my slow-witted przyjaciele?"

Borys, the portly brother with the big head, appeared beside his effeminate womb-sharing associate Bartek, two pelican-faced gangsters in matching brown leather suit jackets and loud silk shirts with tapered collars. They tongue-kissed each other hello and then gazed down at their caged prey.

"Oh, dzien dobry!" they exclaimed in unison.

Moe leaned into Spunk's ear and whispered, "What'd they say?"

"They expressed surprise and then they bid us good day."

"Oh, these muthas wanna play?"

"Yes," Bartek said gleefully from his perch on the boathouse roof, giggling like a schoolgirl. "We loves American games. Especially the rat in a cage."

Borys corrected his brother: "Kot oraz mysz."

"Yes, yes. The pussy and the rat."

"Yeah, yeah," Spunk said. "We already know why you weird fucks are here, but Uncle Cousin Debbie... why? I thought we was solid."

"Thought ya didn't remember me before last night?"

"Not really... but we had one bastard of a time, didn't we?"

Uncle Cousin Debbie smiled broadly. "We did."

Their smile faded swiftly, replaced by grief. "Until you get ripped and run your mouth about who I am and what I am. You know why you don't remember me? Because my dead name is Joe."

"Joe?" Spunk said. Then a light bulb went on

behind his dim eyes. "Joe Some-shit? You Joe Some-shit?" Spunk turned to Moe. "Debbie's the dude I was supposed to meet about the loot!"

Moe shook his head in sheer disbelief.

"You see?" Uncle Cousin Debbie cried. "You got no respect for the transgender community! Never did!"

"But you a cock-swingin' drag queen, Debbie!"

Uncle Cousin wrung their fists so hard their press-on claws got lodged under the skin of their palms.

"I'm pre-op, cocksucker!"

"Cuzz, you get us outta this one and Moe will take care of that nip tuck for ya."

Uncle Cousin Debbie shook their head.

Spunk was beginning to get the sort of look he typically developed in elevators and other small places. It was the look of a feral animal prone to pouncing.

"Listen to me, Poz Nancy Brothers." Spunk glanced at Moe and the two shared a laugh. "Whatever the hell your dummkopf name is. Let us outta here, ya got damn sissies, before we get mad."

"You're not getting out, Spanky."

The voice came as a shock to Spunk who wasn't accustomed to hearing it at such a pitched volume. Brainiac was usually a soft-spoken gentleman, one perpetually preoccupied with the book or paper in his lap. Now, his voice carried more urgency and malice. That's when Spunk noticed that the Brain was the only one still wearing his cuts. Brainiac looked up from a dog-eared copy of Free to Choose by Milton and Rose Friedman, and fixed Spunk with a tired expression.

"Give 'em the till from our run and maybe they don't head up the coast and molest your old ladies in the most indelicate of ways."

"Like with a buzz saw?" Bones asked.

"Yes, Bones," Brainiac replied irritably. "With a buzz saw or broken wine bottle or other implement of torture. Any saw-like item of equal or greater severity."

"You gotta be shitting me," Moe exclaimed.

"No one's shitting you," Brainiac promised. "Unless you're soiling yourself."

"You little rat prick!"

"How juvenile," Brainiac intoned, rolling his eyes. "As if we didn't live in a dog eat dog society. What kinda MC is this after all? You're the first motorcycle club with morals?"

"No," Moe said. "But we have a sense of allegiance and you just trampled on our personal code."

"I do apologize," Brainiac replied unconvincingly. "Bartek, lower the ladder."

There was no movement from overhead. The air was still and you could hear the faint sound of a loon on the other side of the bay door. Everyone looked up and saw that Bartek and Borys were quietly smiling down at them, saying nothing and, yet, speaking volumes.

"Bart!" Brainiac yelled. The ladder. "Throw it down! This is boring me."

All looked up again, but no ladder was forthcoming. Finally, Borys exhaled cigar smoke and handed his hot wet stub off to his brother, who took it enthusiastically, wedging it between his massive pearl white teeth.

"You're all theirs, big mouth." Borys looked from Brainiac over to Spunk. "Consider it parting gift, old man."

"Yes," Bartek grinned. "Like your American Bart Simpson say, 'Go have a town, man!'"

Borys shook his head and seized his brother by

the collar.

Brainiac watched in dismay as his former brothers surrounded him, their eyes full of betrayal and blood lust. He made a mad dash for the bay door, slipping and sliding on the blood and entrails of the disemboweled prospects, but before he could reach for that impossible escape, the bay doors began to close. He looked up and caught sight of Uncle Cousin Debbie plunging a button on a remote. The bay slammed shut and all hands were upon him, tearing at his cuts and his hair and his flesh.

"No weapons," Borys demanded. "We want a nice clean fight."

"Ya ain't gotta worry about that," Spunk assured him. Then he turned back and caught Brainiac in the face with his knee.

Brainiac's nose was slit straight down the middle, causing a pint of blood to leap out and spray him across his forehead. He staggered and whirled around as each Filthy Marauder took his turn using Brainiac's torso as a bag of grain. The wet percussion mallet sound of knuckles crashing into lacerated facial arteries made for a pronounced counterpoint to the crumpled chip bag noises of ribs grinding into splinters and arms fracturing into wedges. Mr. Know-It-All was fast becoming Mr. Broke-It-All.

Bones and Scalps and Foxie Bonnie White struck Brainiac until their bodies gave out and they could strike no more. Spunk and Moe kept going. When one of them would lose steam, the other would pick up where the last had left off. They battered the turncoat until his coat literally turned around and tore into bloodied tatters. Spunk was the last one hunched over his body and the last one to thwack him good and hard in what was left of his head. He wound up and punched clean through the back of Brainiac's skull, ensnaring himself in the process.

"Moe," Spunk said. "Give me a hand."

"I gave you both," Moe insisted.

"Nah, brother. I'm stuck. Got my arm trapped in this sucking head wound."

Moe struggled to his feet and freed Spunk's arm from Brainiac's ruined skull. He held the traitor's body up by the hair and peered inside. The two marveled at the concave cranium before them. For all his talk, all his philosophizing and pseudo-intellectual condescension, there wasn't a whole lot going on upstairs. Spunk looked around the room for evidence of grey matter, but could find none. Moe used the toes of his boots to move the gore around at their feet, but there wasn't so much as a trace of Brainiac's brains.

"Ain't that about a bitch," Moe said. "Brainy fuckin' mouth. Empty fuckin' head."

He and Spunk tossed Brainiac's mangled body aside and looked up to their captors.

"Aight, how about it, Poznanski?"

Borys laughed.

"You must be joking."

"We killed our guy and we got your loot."

"How do you figure?"

"It's right in here. The turncoat's been keepin' it warm for us."

Borys looked dumbfounded and so, too, did the other Filthy Marauders.

"Warm where?" Borys asked.

"Not so quick," Spunk insisted. "We good or what?"

"Fuck no, we're not good. You stole from the Poznanski Brothers and you insult our Polish heritage."

"How? By callin' you a couple of fuckin' dumbbells? If you never heard someone call you that before then you're deaf and dumb."

"Enough lip," Borys snapped. "You're all dead unless you can win the games."

"What games?"

***

Moe had been right about the grid in the floor. The pattern was a track laid in place, which rose up to divide the members of the Filthy Marauders MC. Once the dividers were up, Bartek's words from earlier made more sense; they were trapped in a multichambered zinc-lined pit fashioned from chicken wire and electrodes. Put more simply, the Filthy Marauders were about to play a game of cat and mouse, though it was unclear whether each of them would prove to be the pussy or the rat.

"Ladies first," Borys barked and a door behind the wall shook with the echoing sound of multiple tiny foot falls.

"What the fuck is that?" Foxie Bonnie White cried, her bulging eyes darting around her closed-off unit.

"That's the hoof beats of a thousand rats come to get groovy with your booty," Bartek said.

"Oh, my God!" she cried.

"Of course, you have chance," Borys said.

"What?"

"We'll let the others go if they give you up. Then we can call off the rats and have some real fun."

"Take her!" Scalps said without thinking.

"Yeah," Bones shouted. "Take the bitch! I barely know her! She fucked up my taxes last year!"

"You pencil-necked piece a shit," Foxie Bonnie White howled.

"No!" Spunk shouted.

"You ain't takin' our girl," Moe agreed. "You already turned our boy against us and turned us against him. That's reason enough we should be square."

"You want to be square, you give us ass," Borys said.

"You didn't hear my brother?" Spunk asked. "We said we ain't givin' up anyone."

"We can take her by force," Bartek assured them.

"I'd like to see your jive asses try," Foxie Bonnie declared.

"Very well," Borys said. "Let the games commence."

"Nah," Bones interjected in his nasally voice. "Never send a woman to do a man's job."

"What is this?" Borys demanded. "Chivalry? You're supposed to be dirty! You're supposed to be the meanest men in the world."

Bones bent down and picked up the bottom half of one of the prospects, biting clean through the boy's intestines. The Poznanskis leered at him, grimacing, Bartek gagging.

"What?" Bones whined. "We could be down here for days. A man's gotta fortify himself."

"You're all sick," Bartek cried.

"We're not sick, we're filthy!"

The remaining Marauders howled in solidarity and stomped their boots on the hard wood floor.

"Then you're going to love what you got coming to you," Borys grinned.

He motioned to Uncle Cousin Debbie where she held a remote control in one hand and a cigar in the other.

"No," Debbie said. "Do it ya damn self, I'm havin' a smoke."

Uncle Cousin Debbie tossed the remote to Borys who caught it nervously. He gazed down at Bones and grinned again, plunging a red button with his thumb.

A slat opened in the wall and in poured no fewer than twelve dozen fat rodents, their tails as thick as key lime pie and their beaks stained brown with blood. They swarmed Bones' milky legs, gnawing at his toes and chomping into his varicose veins.

"What the hell is this?" he cried.

"This is Round One of the Dirty Rooster Fuck-off," Borys announced. "Each of you will have a chance to play and each of you will have your chance to die."

"So, what?" Bones yowled, slapping the rodents away from his ankles and trying to fling them off with all of his flailing. "I'm supposed to kill these things?"

"Didn't you hear name of game?" Borys asked.

"The Dirty Rooster Fuck-off," Bartek interjected excitedly.

"Your clothes aren't the only thing that is gone, my friends. Each of you has had their virtue stolen, as well."

"Shit, I had my virtue stolen in sixth grade," Foxie Bonnie White said. "What else ya got?"

The men were less cavalier, save for Spunk.

"I popped my anal cherry when I was eight years old. Fell on a neighbor's wrought-iron fence and cracked my grundle in half."

"Well," Borys said. "Where your virtue used to be, you have been fitted with something much fishier."

"Oh, no!" Bones whimpered, reaching into his gaping asshole and dragging out what looked like a giant slug strangled by tiny tusks and oozing gelatin. In reality, it was a large frozen flounder, half-crushed and thawing fast. Its bones protruded through its mangled gray flesh as it melted out of his butt hole.

"Got damn!" Bones exclaimed, pulling the wretched thing from his body. "I feel like my old lady on her period."

"Maybe now you'll learn how to respect a lady," Uncle Cousin Debbie yelled down at him.

Bones sneered up at them. "Go fumigate yourself, craphead!"

Spunk didn't like anyone talking down to his boys, not even in the literal sense. "Why don't you come down here and I'll give you that sex change you want?"

"I reckon not," Uncle Cousin Debbie said, puffing on her Dutchmaster.

"I'm gonna cut your bowels out and slow roast them shits," Moe promised.

"Enough!" Borys hollered. "Let the games begin!"

Borys hit another switch on the remote and a section of the boathouse wall came away. This served as an invitation for another mischief of rats to scurry in at full speed.

"Holy Schlitz!" Bones cried, recoiling until his back hit the chicken wire. The electrodes sent a quick jolt through his body, which buckled his knees as the rats crowded around his bare ankles. "What the fuck is this!"

"The rules of the Dirty Rooster Fuck-off are simple," Borys explained. "Fuck 'em or flay 'em."

"I'm not fuckin' these harbingers of disease!" Bones insisted, beating the nearest rats away with the oversize flounder in his slippery grip.

"Don't be modest," Borys demanded. "You're the Filthy Marauders. These bastions of filth are your breakfast, lunch, and dinner."

"I stuck my dick in a lot of nasty gash, but I ain't about to stick it in no Black Plague."

"Make your decision," Borys barked.

"Dag gum mother fuck," Bones snapped as the rats began chomping at his feet.

"I ain't fuckin' these things on principle, pig-fucker! Because your simple ass told me to! You want to see blood? I'll show you blood!"

Bones stomped wildly, crushing several rats beneath his size twelve feet. Still, they crawled up his legs and nipped at his genitals. He grabbed them off and squeezed them in his fists, wringing one of them out like a wet wash cloth before stuffing it into his mouth and baring down with his molars. Flecks of gore and gray hair peppered his goatee as he chewed vigorously and swatted at the mischief at his feet.

The wall opened up and another mischief scurried in, trailing their siblings' blood with their big pink feet. Again, Bones stomped like mad and grabbed them up, gnawing off their heads and spitting them at each other.

"Let us out!" he screamed with his mouth full, but Borys did not budge.

The hindquarters of a particularly large rat wriggled back and forth between Bones' jaws, so he clamped down harder, his eyes squeezed shut as he willed his mandible to cut clean through the rodent. Then he reached down and seized the biggest rat of the bunch and shoved it into his face at a horizontal angle, sticking it in his maw like he was gnawing on some corn on the cob.

As the rat's integuments emptied out of its swollen body and leached down the stubbled estuary of Bones' cleft chin, he attempted to broker their release, begging and cursing and pleading. As he screamed with his mouth full, he began choking and one ill-advised gasp was all it took. The rats' remains stopped up his windpipe and Bones fell to the zinc-lined floor in a fit as his lungs searched for air that was not forthcoming.

As Bones' body grew still, his brothers and sister in the MC stared on in muted horror. It wasn't long before movement returned in the form of a mutilated rat making an escape route down Bones' throat and out of his chest cavity. Unfortunately for the rodent, it found its escape hatch was not an escape at all. It was back in the bloody zinc-lined trap with the others. There was no release save for death.

***

"I can do it," Scalps promised them. "I got the equipment."

He pulled out his hunting knife and brandished it proudly, then locked eyes with the largest, nastiest rat in the vicinity.

"Let's dance, Ratatouille!"

Scalps slashed crazily at the air, catching rat after rat as if the whole thing had been choreographed ahead of time. The others watched in shock as he cut a path through the mischief. When the final rat lay motionless and covered in gashes, Scalps crouched down to paw at his wounded ankles. The makeshift toupee he'd been wearing was hanging off his head by a thread. As he nursed his foot, it slid off and landed in the gore. That's when he looked at the fat rat's body and decided it was time to trade up. He took the serrated edge of his knife and bore into the rat's body, sawing hard and fast until he'd removed its hide. Then he placed the warm, wet pelt on the top of his head and smiled.

"Papa's got a brand new bag."

Uncle Cousin Debbie offered a slow clap in response, which prompted Bartek to follow suit.

"Thass American innovation right there," Uncle Cousin Debbie said. "Well done, Scalps."

"Yes," Bartek said. "Well done, Scalps."

Borys nudged his brother hard in the ribs.

"Knock that shit off, pęk!"

"Congratulations," Borys intoned. "You've advanced to Round Two."

"Round Two?" Scalps exclaimed.

"What kinda bullshit is that?" Moe growled.

"The kind of shit that comes out of beavers."

"Beaver," Spunk laughed.

Moe looked over at him and they both grinned.

"Shit," Moe said. "I can handle five beavers at once."

Borys grinned, too, a sinister grin. "We'll see about that, Mohel."

Borys hit another button, which triggered another segment of the wall to retract. This time there was no rush of a mischief but the slow, heavy padding of large webbed feet and thick scale-covered tails.

"That don't sound like no beaver I ever tamed," Moe mused.

"Fuck me sideways," Scalps declared as he came face to face with a colony of hundred pound beavers. They stomped up before him, whisking and flexing their long, sharp nails. The beavers' thick, wet fur gave off an odor that said it had already tasted blood and wanted more.

"How the fuck?" Spunk cried in sheer awe.

"Wisconsin beaver," Borys said. "The biggest beaver colony ever recorded. An average of one hundred and ten pounds each. Big ole fat beavers for our big ole fat friends."

"You cunt!" Scalps cursed, but before he could say anything more the first of the beavers was on him, munching through his balls with its long gnawing teeth. His hand went for his knife, but the second beaver knocked it free, crunching on his wrist until his hand dangled from a thin cord of ligament.

"Kill these fuckin' things!" he screamed.

Moe swung a length of chain at the biggest one, connecting with its flat head, but this did not seem to faze it, as it continued to attack Scalps with its clawed front feet and massive incisors.

"Kill 'em!" he cried as the biggest of the colony burrowed into his exposed clavicle, feeding on raw nerves and muscle. The second beaver chewed on his arm, while the others circled his feet in a frenzy, lapping at his blood as it fell in great splashes of bright red.

Foxie Bonnie White drew their attention by swinging her garters at them.

"C'mon, you little creeps! Let me show you what a real beaver looks like!"

She crouched down and removed her g-string, then used it like a sling shot to hit the largest of the beavers in its face. Her plan worked. The beaver stopped its gnawing at Scalps and its eyes darted over to the half-naked Filipino girl with the scallop-shaped pubic 'fro.

"Come and get locked in my heart-shaped box."

The colony beat a hasty retreat from the maimed Scalps, cutting under the electrified chicken wire and getting shocked in the process. Undisturbed by the zaps, the monstrous rodents surrounded the still-squatting Foxie Bonnie. This was all the distraction they needed.

Gary leaped over his side of the chicken wire

and landed, nude, behind the beavers. His giant, scarred hands reached out and seized the largest of the beavers from behind. He took its stout hindquarters in his Vise-like grip, yanked its flat tail aside, and thrust his cock into its dewy hole.

The rest of the colony paid no mind to this assault, as Foxie Bonnie White lured them into her honey trap, hooking a finger slowly and seductively in the direction of her blood-moistened meat curtains. As they approached with teeth bared, she parted her lips and leaned back, making room for the beasts in her box.

Gary pounded the King Beaver as hard as his hips would go, punching it in his side with one fist for every thrust. As he neared completion, he reached around and grabbed the beaver by its chisel-like teeth and pulled back.

"Give up that castoreum, you furry sonovabitch!"

Foxie Bonnie clamped shut with all the force of her kegels, suffocating the entire batch of bastard beavers, her frail body jiggling back and forth as they attempted to back out of their ill-fated burrow. She crossed her legs like her mama used to tell her to and then twisted around, refusing them any chance of a getaway.

As the hideous head rodent gooed all over Gary's johnson, he yanked his arm back, stripping the beaver for parts like an old jalopy. Ejaculate trickled down his inner thighs and he stood, dazed, on trembling legs, holding the skull and spine of the freshly fucked, freshly skinned semi-aquatic rat in his fist.

"Did I win?" he asked.

"No," Foxie Bonnie said, assuming a cowpoke gait. "I did."

That's when four sopping wet beaver carcasses

issued forth from her cavernous vagina. They slid slug-slow down her inner thigh before hitting the floor coated in pussy juice. The way their wet fur corpses inched out of her cunt hole you'd have thought she was giving birth to a lot of costume Yosemite Sam mustaches. When the final pelt slapped against the musty floor, Foxie Bonnie's bulbous lips slowly returned to their former glory.

"What's next?" she asked.

ONE FINAL FUCK YOU

The Poznanskis hadn't expected the gang to last this long, especially not with weapons still in their possession. Bart's money had been on them throwing their weapons away.

They'll fire all their bullets and throw all their chains in our direction and then they'll have nothing, he'd thought.

Borys figured they would all beg for death once they'd mislaid their knives and chains. Still, he planned ahead in the event that they survived the second round, which is why he saved the worst for last.

"I bet you're all wondering, 'Why does he call it the Dirty Rooster Fuck-off?'"

"Nope," Foxie Bonnie White said, taking a long pull off a spliff.

"Not once," Gary said.

"You jive mutha," Moe snapped. "Our friends lyin' over here with his chest meat out. You think we give a wet fuck about the inspiration behind your sadistic game show bullshit? Get the fuck on!"

Spunk laughed and looked up with a sneer. "Sorry, Fuckface! Not the answer you was lookin' for, sweetie?"

Borys's chest heaved as he stink-eyed his biker rival.

"All the same," he intoned bitterly. "You should know ... we saved the worst for last."

"Isn't that considerate," Moe said, catching the

spliff as Foxie Bonnie threw it to him and sticking it between his gap-toothed grin.

Spunk craned his neck, attempting to look beyond the Polacks to their ole pal Uncle Cousin.

"Cuzz!" he yelled. "Hey, Cuzz! You up still up there?"

"Yeah, why?" came a distant, begrudging reply.

"We got sumpin' to say."

"So, say it."

"C'mon, now. Lemme see a bitch before I gotta fuck a nematode or whatever these dipshits got in mind fer us."

A hoarse sigh came from somewhere up on the rooftop. After a moment, Uncle Cousin Debbie appeared by the brothers' side.

"I'm fine," Debbie assured Borys.

"Make it quick," he said.

Debbie peered over the side at Spunk. He looked like a child despite the long, thinning hair, and the graying beard. He looked up sheepishly from beneath his droopy eyelids and swayed from hip to hip, uncertain about what to say.

"Well?" Debbie asked.

Spunk looked to Moe, at a loss. Moe shrugged.

Uncle Cousin Debbie shifted their feet impatiently and rested a palm on their hip.

"I'm losing patience, boys."

"Debbie," Spunk started, clearing his throat. "Uh... we don't talk shit because you a woman born trapped in a man's body. We talk shit because you a inbred mutant with teeth in ya forehead and breath like ya paw jus birthed you out his poop chute."

Moe looked up, adding quickly, "What Spunk means is, you one of us, darlin.'"

"The fuck I do!" Spunk insisted. "Traitorous bitch!"

"C'mon now," Moe insisted, eyes bugging out.

"C'mon now. Come correct."

Uncle Cousin Debbie grit their teeth and chucked their cigar over the side, then started away.

"Naw," Spunk insisted, crossing his arms and pouting.

"Girl," Moe called out, drawing Uncle Cousin's attention. "You know the Filthy Marauders cum on everyone's back, regardless of they reproductive equipment."

Uncle Cousin Debbie smiled. Moe winked. Spunk chanced a peek in Debbie's direction and was strangely taken by their smile. He could faintly remember their time together on bath salts.

"Thass right," he said. "And didn't I drink them balls, Cuzz?"

"Yeah," Uncle Cousin Debbie laughed, lighting another cigar nervously.

"And I rimmed that o-ring a yours like it was my own," said Moe.

"A surprise to no one," Spunk replied. He beamed up at Uncle Cousin Debbie, batting his eyelashes. "What do ya say, Cuzz?"

"I say, 'Y'all so full a shit, you names should be Huggies and Luvs.'"

Uncle Cousin Debbie pulled an ivory-handled pistol from their mud-stained fur coat and trained it on the men below.

"Motherhumper!" Spunk spat.

"Do what you're told," Debbie demanded.

"Right," Spunk said, smiling. "We always freakin' at the freaker's ball."

Uncle Cousin Debbie sucked their tooth and started away, a thousand yard stare on their stubbly face.

"It was worth a shot," Moe said.

"Yeah," Spunk said, reaching into his jacket and pulling out an empty shot glass. He set it down on the floor and slid it to Gary. "Shot a cum maybe. I'm parched."

***

Spunk thought he could hear a chorus in the distance, a large chorus worthy of an orchestra. Its voices were far away and blended together into one big voice that seemed to grow bigger and shriller the closer it came. He thought he could hear the chorus mocking him.

"Fuck off! Fuck off! Fuck off!" the chorus cried.

"Do you hear that?" Spunk asked no one in particular.

"My stomach be grumblin' too if I just drank a half gallon of Gary."

The depleted prospect shook his head.

"I hear it too," he said. "It's behind the wall."

"FUCK OFF! FUCK OFF! FUCK OFF! FUCK OFF!"

"It's getting louder," Foxie Bonnie exclaimed.

Borys grinned wickedly: "That's the whole world laughing at you, you czarnuch cipka!"

"I know this mutha didn't just drop an N bomb followed by the C word."

"What are we in kindergarten?" Spunk said. "Also, I think it's technically two C words in this case, no?"

Moe shook his head and leered at the Poznanski Brothers.

"What is it, you jive-ass bird turd? You got some other muthafuckas here wanna fuck wit us?"

"Indeed, we do," Borys confirmed. "

"FUCK OFF! FUCK OFF! FUCK OFF! FUCK OFF!"

"I'd like to introduce you to the Dragon Chicken. You'll have to excuse their manners. They have never been this far west of Vietnam."

Moe's eyes ignited at this mention of the east and of Nam in particular.

Borys hit one of his little buttons and the wall opened up again. In came a throng of fat Southeast Asian chickens with engorged feet and wattles the size of human tongues. Now, the choir was at full volume and the acoustics of the boathouse caused their clucks to mingle into one continuous chorus.

"FUCKOFFFUCKOFFFUCKOFFFUCKOFFFUC KOFFFUCKOFFFUCKOFFFUCKOFF!!!"

"We have the finest cocks you could ask for," Bartek announced, smiling broadly.

Borys pinched the bridge of his nose, clearly at his wit's end with his brother.

"Holy fuck," Foxie Bonnie exclaimed. "These cocks are huge!"

"What do we do?" Gary asked, looking to the elder statesmen for advice.

Spunk and Moe could do nothing but marvel at the awe-inspiring size of the flock and their hideous waddles as they dragged on the ground.

"I think I'm gonna ralph," Spunk admitted.

"You'll want to watch that," Borys yelled down. "We've starved these prized cocks since their last fight... three days ago. You put anything in front of them and they'll devour it."

"FUCKOFFFUCKOFFFUCKOFFFUCKOFFFUC KOFFFUCKOFFFUCKOFF!!!"

The gang could tell they were done in. Fucked over. Destined for failure. The fat little peckers had them outnumbered. They could either lie down and get pecked to death or leave this stinking world the same way they'd lived in it—sucking, spitting, stabbing, fucking, and slurping every drop of blood, sweat, and cum that they could. Foxie Bonnie White gave them the kick in the ass they needed by taking the lead and hurling herself crotch first onto the biggest cock she saw. She'd heard about what happens when you cut off one of these fuckers' heads, but she was about to find out what happened when you blindfolded one deep within the folds of your twat.

Her pussy swallowed the chicken's head in one shot and the creature's red comb tickled her clit as she rode it around their makeshift pen. The crest was biting into her cervix as its spurs began buckling. She rode the feathered fuck like a mechanical bull and did her best to sucker punch the other chickens in her wake as it gobbled about.

Gary was kicking the chicken shit clean out of two of the meanest cocks in the room, a pair of muscled Sumatra chickens. When the pair dropped momentarily, he thought he'd felled the beasts. No dice. They turned around and lashed him across his eyes with their tail feathers, sending him staggering back into the chicken wire. Gary took a shock so strong and prolonged it dropped him like a sack of laundry. His jeans filled with diarrhea and his body went limp.

Spunk watched this go down and felt a paternal sense of concern.

"Gary! Good gracious! What in the good got damn is that smell, boy?"

Gary's flaccid body sagged against a barrel of chum as the smaller chickens nipped at his legs.

"I shit my britches," he admitted.

Spunk kicked the little cocks away from his young friend's legs and started pulling at his jeans.

"What are ya doin?'" Gary asked.

"I'm using your unfortunate situation to our advantage," Spunk insisted.

"How?"

"You went veggies only on account a you heard

Foxie Bonnie was a vegan, right?"

"Yeah."

"So, have you actually stuck to the vegan diet?"

"Mostly," Gary said.

"Good," Spunk smiled. "Then this should work like gangbusters."

Spunk pulled Gary's jeans off carefully.

"Dude, what are you doing? I just shit."

"I know," Spunk said. "Now let's find out if we can trust what we read in National Geographic."

Spunk took the Wranglers full of the runs and flung them at the flock of chickens nearest to them. As the Filthy Marauders' veep had hoped, the chickens were fond of the herbivorous excrement.

"Look at that," he said. "You and these cocks have somethin' in common. You both eat flowers and weeds."

They could see Moe tangling with a Shamo chicken in the corner, taking blows in the chest from its abnormally long neck. Spunk struggled to help Gary to his feet, but their attention was redirected when Foxie Bonnie White wailed from the opposing corner. The disoriented chicken with its head in Foxie's heart-shaped box had staggered right into a mosh pit of his fellow cocks, which sent Foxie Bonnie White flying right into a bevy of bloodthirsty beaks. They were on her in synchronized action, pecking the fuck out of her arms, chest, and abdomen, until she stopped fighting and fell still.

Seeing this, Gary roared in anguish, which distracted the Shamo chicken long enough for Moe to seize it by its throat. He opened his mouth wide and bit the chicken's head off, spitting it at the flock of birds with their beaks in Foxie Bonnie's blood. Then he turned the cock upside down and choked up on its long neck like a bat. His eyes locked on the biggest, ugliest chickens around Foxie Bonnie's stomach and swung with all his might. Feathers went flying and the fearsome fowl shot up, hitting the Poznanski Brothers in their matching sheepskin mountaineer hats.

Gary dropped to his knees by Foxie Bonnie's side, sobbing and drooling by her motionless body. Moe watched this and gritted his teeth, reaching the point of exasperation. Spotting his bike where it was propped against one of the boathouse's barrels, Moe made up his mind. It was time to take one for the team, lest they end up stuck in there to rot forever with Vietnamese poultry monsters. With all the force he could muster, he sprang off the balls of his feet, lunging across the electrified divider. The metal barbs sunk deep into his gut, tearing flesh during his descent.

If he stretched forward about an inch and a quarter he could reach the saddlebag on the side of his bike. In so doing, he would surely rupture a vital organ, but if he didn't do anything except hang there from the divider, the chicken wire would almost certainly sink deeper and deeper into his flesh until it did the job for him.

His head bobbed around, taking in the scene as it remained—Foxie Bonnie White down for the count, his brothers in bondage ripped open as if they were frogs in a science lab, and his main man Spunk at sixes and sevens over the whole damn thing. From where he was dangling, he could see something that Gary couldn't: shallow breaths beneath the orange, pink, and green "Flower Power" bralette, breaths just strong enough to convince him that there were still some people left dying for. As Gary cried gritty tears and the Poznanski Brothers argued over who got to control the remote overhead, Moe rocked forward as hard as he could until the skin on his left flank gave away and he landed on the other side of the fence, one hand gripping his side as it spilled open and the other reaching madly for his pannier.

Spunk was busy working out the mathematics of the boathouse, how many barrels there were in all. The cat he'd talked to on the phone said big money. Promised at least a quarter million or more. The barrels' size suggested there was more, but getting to one to count it was another story. As Borys laced into Bartek about behaving like a big boy, Spunk crept toward the closest one and attempted to lean over the chicken wire to get himself a peak. That's when he heard the noise, a wire hanger on harpsichord sound that set his hair standing on end. His eyes shot across the room in time to see Moe staggering back in his direction, a hand grenade held aloft and his steaming innards slopping out onto the floor.

"Hey, Poznanski," he said, clutching his side and wincing as viscera dangled down his leg and blood pumped out of him like a fast-draining swimming pool. "You heard the one about the Polish loan shark?"

The Poznanskis looked down at him and flashed their gold teeth at him. Borys shrugged, effectively playing along.

Moe winced as he continued: "Ggle lent out all his money... skipped town."

Silence came from the rafters.

"No?" Moe said as he grew dizzy and his fingers shook. "Maybe you'll like this one. What do ya do if a Polack throws a hand grenade at you?"

The brothers stared at him, saying nothing.

"C'mon," Moe said. "Play along."

Borys rolled his eyes. "Fine, fine. What do you do Polak throws hand grenade?"

"Take the pin out and throw it back."

The brothers stared at Moe, uncomprehending and angry. Then the pair looked at each other, searching each others faces for the answer to a riddle that did not exist.

"Take the pin out and throw it back," Moe repeated.

Borys shoved his brother, then his brother shoved him. Each of them figured the other was keeping the secret of the joke to himself.

"Take the pin out and throw it back," Moe repeated again, smiling through the tears.

This time, he wound up like he was Satchel Paige, and chucked a fast ball at the rooftop. The grenade landed on the industrial shingles of the roof and rolled to the spot where Borys and Bartek's cheap leather shoes met one another. The dastardly duo looked down, slack-jawed, at the green iron egg.

"It's real!" Bartek exclaimed. "No joke! It's real!"

"Watch out, you imbecile!"

Borys attempted to push his brother out of harm's way, but Bart took this as a personal affront. He shoved his brother back.

"O cholera!" Borys screamed, jumping back and shielding his head.

The bang went up, blinding all in the boathouse, and leaving a hole in the roof big enough to fit a Buick. Rubble rained down on Spunk who braced himself in much the same fashion as Borys. If this were a morality play, now would be the time for Borys and Spunk to share a warm cup of hot cocoa, while waxing philosophical about their fundamental commonalities, and how they won out over the intrinsic evils of a society that marginalizes the criminally insane. Instead, all you're gonna get is some gore and, maybe, a head full of gratuitous nudity.

***

The blast had maimed Bart, but he didn't seem to notice. His brother had a harder time looking at his fresh wounds than he did bearing their pain.

"You fool," Borys said, punching his brother in his shredded shoulder. "You could have been killed! As it stand, you look like golabki!"

"What do you?" Bartek said, shoving Borys with his working arm. "Heh? Ale jest, jak jest."

Bartek's dead arm hung at his side, covered in flaps of torn fabric and skin. His upheaval looked especially comical with his lame arm, as if you were watching an awkward open mic night performance. A hole had been burned clear through his slacks, so that his shriveled and badly scarred schmeckle was on full display. Borys caught this and had a fit.

"Put your penis away, Bartek! What would papa say? Hmm! What would papa say!"

"Enough! Ala jest, jak jest!"

Borys slapped his brother in the face.

"Stop saying!"

"Son of a bitch," Gary said, shaking shreds of roof shingles out of his matted hair. "I think I'm deaf."

Spunk didn't answer, only stared down at the pile that used to be his best friend. Moe was uncooked sausage, curled up on the floor with his entrails coiled all about him. Spunk couldn't recognize his brother any more. He imagined this was what dogs must feel like when their owners go away forever and then show back up a husk from having worked all day at some square job. The corpse on the floor was some poor wax museum facsimile of the fella who'd been his ride or die for the last twenty years.

"It was good riding with you, Morris," he said under his breath. "Save me some shine on the Devil's time."

Gary walked to the edge of the divider as the Poznanskis argued overhead. "Fucking sucks balls about Moe, man."

Spunk grumbled. "The ball suckin' is done, son."

"She's breathing," Gary said, hooking a thumb in Foxie Bonnie White's direction. "If she's gonna make it we need to get the fuck outta Dodge."

"How'd you like to do that, son? You got another load in you? Pretty sure the game ain't over yet."

"Right you are, Mr. Mahoney!" Borys looked down on the two men still standing and grinned iniquitously. "The Dirty Rooster Fuck-Off is about to begin."

"What the fuck?" Gary shouted. "What the fuck we been doin' here all along? Playin' pocket pool?"

"Think of it as rehearsal," Borys suggested. "Now you join major leagues."

***

The wall opened as it had before, but there was no sound of scurrying cocks coming in a colony. No buk buk bukaw chorus of fuck-offs from a colony of angry birds. The room was silent save for an intermittent stomping sound that grew closer and closer until, finally, the Filthy Marauders could see the Poznanskis' weapon of mass destruction in all of its feathered fury. Its mean, pointy spurs stuck out longer than a horned up teenager's hard-on and its hard outer layer appeared sharper than any knife the Marauders had brought with them.

The rooster's red eyes fixed on Spunk, rheumy and deranged, evil and insane. Its gaze was inhuman and full of an angst no doubt borne of its upbringing. Lord knows what the Polaks had been doing to break the thing, but whatever it was it had worked. The creature that stood before them possessed a singular purpose—pure unbridled assault. As it fluffed its enormous saddle feathers, its eyes went to the roof, seeking approval from its master. Borys stared down with a paternal smile on his face.

"Not so stupid now, are we, Spanky?"

"Yeah, ya fuckin' are," Spunk laughed. "You two puddinheaded Polacks gotta be thicker than a polar bear's foreskin. You thought we was rollin' in here with our cocks flappin' in the wind letting some strange cunt dump barrels of hooch down our throats... without us having back?"

Borys gaped at him, utterly befuddled.

Spunk motioned to Gary. "Wake up the Trog."

"You said you wasn't gonna bring it," Gary snapped. "I told you it'd suffocate."

"Let's see," Spunk grinned defiantly. "You better bet you was wrong."

Gary reached into his pocket and pulled out a quarter. He trained it at Moe's bike and hurled it good and hard. The quarter whizzed through the air and dinged against the front of Moe's side car. A wooden crate sat in the side car seat, chained but unlocked. Something stirred from within then went silent.

Spunk smiled. "Guess you was wrong after all, boy."

Gary stared at the side car with mouth agape.

"G'awn," Spunk instructed. "Give 'em his wake-up call."

"Dick cheese," Gary shouted.

The room was silent. Borys exchanged a smirk with his brother as Uncle Cousin Debbie appeared to stare down the opening in the roof.

"Dick cheese!" Gary commanded.

The Trog broke free from the wooden crate holding him and rose up with some difficulty until he stood, monolithic and buck naked, over Moe's bike.

Spunk grinned proudly. "Troggy here only looks like twelve pounds of shit in a five pound bag. He used be one of you meatheads. Till we broke him like the bitch that he is. Now he's our good whittle boy and our dog is fiercely loyal, Borys."

Spunk and the gang had found him digging through their personal possessions while they were getting jumped by a street dealer and his thugs. After they mutilated their attackers and smoked up all their shit, Spunk discovered that buck-toothed man-child chewing on their saddle bags. The Filthy Marauders' weapons and cash were stuffed haphazardly in his pockets. No camouflaging his intention and no syllables in his vocabulary to persuade them otherwise.

Rather than waste some neanderthal right there for abiding his baser instincts, the gang decided to take him back to their club house, and see how much he could take. Spunk and his brothers poured liquor down his throat and beat him senseless, taking care not to bash his brains in before they could test his endurance. Over the ensuing days, the Filthy Marauders took clubs, bottles, chains, and knives to the Trog, but he kept on kicking. When it was obvious what a tough motherfucker the little scamp was, Spunk decided to chain him up in the store room beneath the club. The room was devoid of light or mirrors, which proved influential to the

Trog's bizarre evolution.

You know that old wives' tale about not making funny faces? How if you keep making a hideous expression your face will freeze in that position and you'll look that ugly forever? As it turned out, there was some veracity to the old saw. When the boys started working out on the Trog with their whips and chains, he had looked like your typical dim-witted kid with dumb eyes and a goofy grill. Once the beatings started in earnest he started to screw his face up into terrible grimaces until, eventually, his muscles locked up into some petrified rictus. After they dumped a bucket of battery acid on the son of a bitch, they expected the flesh would melt right off his skull, but the opposite was true. The Trog's head grew until it could fill an industrial garbage bag, which is where they kept it when they weren't feeding or beating him.

As the days bled into weeks and the weeks into months, the Trog continued to mature like an old block of cheese; he grew a green fuzz on his otherwise bald dome and his eyes sunk deep into his head, which only served to accentuate his already cartoonishly large eyes. After one of the gang attempted to put him out of his misery with a broken forty to the skull, his hardened flesh forced the bottle out with a growth that could best be described as a bony stub or calcified horn. It was about that time that Spunk started weight training the poor bastard and the Trog became their secret weapon.

"Our very own unicorn," he used to call him.

For two hours a day, the Trog was allowed out of the dark to drink his fill in moonshine and receive proper training. This training consisted of watching action movies in the club office. Spunk would disengage the security cameras for ninety minutes and stick a VHS tape in the VCR, leaving the Trog glued to the set while he went about MC business. The Trog got a first-class education in the kung-fu moves of Jim "Black Belt Jones" Kelly, the merciless biker vengeance of The Wild Angels, and the equally merciless outlaw justice of The Wild Bunch. Once he'd seen Leo Gorcey in No Holds Barred, Spunk knew he was ready to rock.

The Filthy Marauders invited a rival biker gang to the club to negotiate a stalemate. After some drinks and blow, they brought them to the basement to see their latest haul. The Trog was waiting and, within minutes, their interstate trafficking troubles were over. The man-child tore their enemies from asshole to occipital lobe with his bare hands. Ever since, Spunk had thought of the Trog as a handy tool, kind of like the life insurance policies squares liked to keep. If everything went full shit house, he knew he had the Trog on standby. Now, as the abomination lurched out of the crate and faced off against the giant Essex cockerel in the corner of the room, he wondered if he might have underestimated their secret weapon. Would this massive, monstrous creature be able to stop killing once the cock and the Eurotrash were crushed beneath his big ass feet? It was a chance he had to take.

The Poznanskis looked on in abject horror as the Trog lumbered over to the blinking rooster and seized it by its comb, shoving thirteen inches of throbbing cock meat into the bird's cloaca. Those red beady eyes went wide as it clucked its last. The rooster's throat burst open, showering the Trog's burly chest in blood, guts, and jissom. A quick shudder ran down its saddle feathers as the man-child punched through its neck with his mutant wang. The Trog continued to rock back and forth on his heels, digging his swollen glans into the cockerel's gizzard. As his mutant eyes rolled back in his head and his loins continued to flood the bird's throat, the Trog balled his fists, decimating the rooster's rib cage and effectively compartmentalizing its torso into a whoopee cushion. As the last drop of semen dripped from his ungodly schlong, the Trog took the bird's wattle between his thumb and forefinger and flung it up at the Poznanski Brothers, then started toward the far wall.

The dividers fell away as his titanic thighs ripped right through the chicken wire and he made for a pole leading to the ceiling. Before he could reach his target, Borys pulled out a shotgun and began firing down the hole. The first shot struck the Trog in his chest, blasting off one of his shoulders. The Polak fired again, hitting him in the top of his enormous head. As blood trickled into his feeble eyes, the Trog kept walking with the same singular purpose as his demolished fuck toy.

A shot missed its intended target and grazed the side of Gary's head, shaving off a segment of his dirty blond hair and leaving a waxen burn across the right side of his forehead. Borys steadied himself against the edge of the roof and aimed carefully, pulling the trigger as he exhaled. This was the one that did it. The shot connected with the Trog's leg, obliterating kneecap and femur with one round.

"Suck me silly," Spunk exclaimed in defeat.

The Trog went supine and stock still as the blood gushed out of it.

Spunk knelt down beside him and pressed a warm palm to what was left of his forehead.

"That'll do, Trog."

"Roadhouse?" Trog asked.

"Sure," Spunk said.

The Trog let out a sigh of relief as his irises went white.

"Well, ya got me there," Spunk said.

Borys grinned.

"We got you last night, Spanky. This is merely final ha-ha."

"Hurrah," Spunk corrected.

"Co?"

"Never mind," Spunk spat bitterly. "What's next?"

"You bleed. That's what's next. That's all that's next."

Spunk nodded. "Uh-huh."

***

The vice president of the Filthy Marauders was reconciling himself with the idea that he'd be stone dead within moments. He'd played his last real card and the only trick he had up his sleeve was one based on pure speculation. Was he right? Was the loot they'd driven down to Delacroix to collect really as close as he thought it was? These were the questions swirling around in his skull when his shoulders and chest were suddenly soaked in piss.

He let out a scream and staggered back, shielding his face with his forearms. Borys caught Spunk in his arms, steeping his wrists and fingers in the golden flow.

"Ah, fuck you, man!"

Borys laughed.

"How the hell'm I supposed to enjoy my last Cigarillo I can't even light the got damn thing?"

"You no light, Mr. Mahoney. We turn your lights out."

Borys trained his gun on Spunk and went for

the trigger.

"Hold up now," Spunk said. "Put that piece away. Be a man about this shit at least. Jeez-sauce!"

Borys considered this and thoughtfully placed the handgun in the back of his waist band.

"Tell ya what," Spunk said. "You let us outta this hole and I'll give ya the money we owe. Then you and me, we get down. Whoever's still standing after I wallop your ass, they get to walk. No questions asked."

"How?" Borys asked. "How you expect us to believe you have money? We check before put you in boathouse. Beer money, no big thing. You don't have scooch."

Spunk laughed, both at Borys's poor choice of words and his presumption.

"But we do," Spunk said. "We got your money because your money is our money."

"I don't follow," Borys admitted, his brow deeply furrowed.

"Shock," Spunk said sarcastically. "You're the two hayseeds Joe told us about. Said two idiots were stashin' all they loot in a boathouse."

"We don't stash our money."

"Of course not," Spunk agreed. "You have people to do that for you, right? People like Cuzz up there."

Borys motioned to Bartek who dragged Uncle Cousin Debbie across what remained of the roof.

"Is this true?" he asked them.

Uncle Cousin Debbie looked from Borys down to Spunk and back again. Then they mumbled under their breath. "You told me to put it somewhere no one would look for it."

"Brudny pęk!" Borys cursed.

Spunk's fingers felt around the lid of a barrel, searching for the lock on its hoop.

"Hey Cuzz," he said as he threw the release. "You a big mama. How full did you make these?"

Uncle Cousin Debbie cracked a smile.

"Guess you'll have to see for ya self."

Spunk threw the head off the barrel and peered inside at... shit. A whole lot of it. Borys began laughing hoarsely and stomping his foot.

"You're in some shit as they say."

"No," Spunk said. "No fuckin' way!"

"Run-off from one of our projects. Wastewater treatment plant. Durr City."

"No fuckin' way!" Spunk growled.

He ran to the far end of the room and opened a distant barrel, choking and gagging as he ripped the lid off and found himself slapped in the face with the stank of more human waste. He did it again and again until only one barrel remained.

"Enough of this," Borys sighed, rolling his eyes. "Face it, Spanky. You're in deep shit."

"Fuck you," Spunk spat. "At least let me have the long shot."

Borys gestured in acquiescence as Spunk made for the last of the barrels. With slight hesitation, Spunk removed the head of the final fifty-five gallon drum. Inside, a tall stack of billfolds competed for room with a mess of elicit substances. The drugs were organized by strength, with bricks of Jamaican weed on the bottom, bundles of Afghani horse in the middle, vials of black rock in a sock, and several eight-balls of crank on top.

"Eureka," Spunk declared.

"I don't know why you're excited," Borys said. "We have no deal."

"But we do," Uncle Cousin Debbie said, holding her palm out over the side of the half-demolished roof, and winking at Spunk.

Spunk grinned. "I'll kiss yours if you'll kiss

mine."

"Let's boogie," Debbie said, opening her palm over the hole.

A key sailed through the air on a rabbit's foot parachute. Spunk caught it and knew exactly what to do. He made for his bike where it was braced between two of the shit barrels. He jumped onto the V65 Magna, straddling the pleated pillion sadde, as he jammed the key in the ignition lock.

"Queer stinking kurwa," Borys cursed as he kicked Uncle Cousin Debbie in the ass, sending her over the side of the roof.

Gary rushed across the room, managing to catch Debbie in his arms and sprain his ankles in the process. Cuzz Debbie looked up at the strapping young bruiser and beamed.

"Where have you been all my life?" they said.

"In my daddy's balls," Gary replied.

Satisfied that Debbie was alive, Spunk revved the engine. Borys smirked.

"Think you're big mozzarella now, eh? So fucking what? You're down there and we're up here, and that's always how it's gonna be. We have cast you into abaddon and that's where you stay. You were born to be at the bottom, so stay where you belong."

Spunk scanned the room, studying its dimensions. He then squeezed the back tire of his bike and ran his fingers along the treads. It had been fifteen years since he attempted a Scummy Whirlpool. The last attempt had left him with scar tissue up and down his left flank and thirty-five pins in his legs besides.

"Get dead center," he instructed Gary.

His young charge listened, carefully dragging Foxie Bonnie White's unconscious body to the center of the room while Uncle Cousin Debbie limped along in his wake. They lay down flat on the floor and took a deep breath as Spunk leered at Borys and blipped the Magna's throttle.

"You just down-talked the wrong Chicano, fuckface!"

Before Borys could respond, Spunk busted out with the Scummy Whirlpool, kicking up smoke and then taking the room in laps before hitting the walls in a slow but steady circle. The bike climbed the wall inch by inch with each downshift until he neared the precipice. As Borys reached clumsily for the gun in his waist band, Spunk threw it in sixth gear, squeezed his eyes shut, and let the rear sprockets do their job.

One hundred horses came galloping over the edge of the demolished roof. The fork of the Magna smashed into Bartek's face, which caught on the axle and came off like a bottle top, rolling across the ramshackle shingles. The bike skidded across the roof in a circular pattern as Spunk sat on his bad leg and gave the battlecruiser some more throttle.

Borys jumped back as his brother's disembodied head went rolling over the side of the boathouse. He made for a ladder at the opposite end, scurrying like a rat for perceived safety.

Spunk looked to the far edge of the roof and found another Essex cockerel, this one plumper and meaner than the last, sitting in a cramped cage. The fun wasn't over yet. He grabbed the coop by its makeshift chain handle and headed for the only exit.

The Magna jumped the roof and landed on Borys's back, effectively cushioning Spunk's impact and paralyzing his opponent. As Borys began whining and coughing up blood at his feet, Spunk climbed off the battlecruiser and engaged the kickstand. The engine idled loudly as he set the bird cage down beside Borys and reached inside.

The monster rooster went for his wrist, but Spunk wrapped his fingers around its throat, holding it firmly in place.

"Hungry, boy? Everyone's gotta carb load before a good fuck-off, right?" He brought the bird's head down by Borys's whimpering face and allowed the cock to stare at its supper. "Go on, boy. Bon appetit."

Spunk loosened his grip and the rooster pecked wildly at Borys's face, burrowing at his peeper holes until his eyeballs were a bubbly gelatin. The Polak's wail echoed out across Durr City Creek as the cock ate its fill of his ocular cavities.

The last of the Poznanskis went limp from shock, so Spunk bitch-slapped him awake.

"I know you can't see, but this is your dirty rooster... right?"

Borys groaned in the affirmative, sobbing deeply.

"Well," Spunk said, kicking the rooster in its tail feathers and setting it free. "Allow me to introduce you to my filthy fucking chicken strips!"

Spunk disengaged the kickstand and brought the carcass of his rear tire to rest against Borys's blubbering lips. The treads were jammed into the crook of Borys's mouth where his mandible met his maxilla. He gagged as the black rubber tickled his uvula. Spunk planted both feet firmly on the dirt path beside the boathouse and revved the engine, which caused Borys to gag louder. That's when Spunk wrapped four fingers around the clutch and pulled it back against the handlebar with all his might.

With his free hand, Spunk threw the bike into first gear and twisted the throttle down, watching as the arrow on the Magna's gauge inched toward the red line. He glanced over at Foxie Bonnie White where she hung from Gary's broad neck. She nodded and Spunk nodded in kind, leaning forward and letting the clutch go.

The Magna peeled out, peeling back Borys's epidermis, and thumping in and out of his squamous like it was going over potholes at top speed. A faint red mist was kicked up in the cloud of smoke, caking the Filthy Marauders in a haze of their enemy's life force.

Spunk threw the clutch and rolled back the throttle, then climbed off the bike with much difficulty, his leg locking up as he turned to face his opponent. Sure enough, Borys's head looked like a pile of chicken strips smothered in barbecue sauce. His body was already drawing flies.

"How's that for fuck off?" Spunk spat.

He lumbered over to his compadres and stuck a Cigarillo between his teeth. Gary reached into his pocket and produced a Zippo, allowing the lid to fall back as he thumbed the flint wheel, and lit the vice president's smoke. Spunk took a hard pull, exhaling through his nose like a fierce dragon. His eyes went to the waxen scar on Gary's grill and the absence of hair on that part of his scalp.

"Missing a little off the top," he said.

Gary ran his palm over his still-fresh wound. "No harm done."

"We'll call you Hair Piece, in honor of Scalps."

"Dig it," Gary said, smiling warmly.

Uncle Cousin Debbie had been standing off to the side, but now they approached Spunk tentatively. He locked eyes with them like he was boring a hole. For a moment, Uncle Cousin Debbie expected a knife between the eyes, which made what came next a relief.

"We never saw you on our run," Spunk said.

"Joe Some-Shit was a no-show. You flaked this year, unnerstan?"

"Sounds like me," Uncle Cousin Debbie said, a shit-eating grin smoothing itself across their grizzled face.

They extended their hand for a shake, but Spunk took it in his and planted a wet one on the dorsal side.

"I knew you was a gentleman," Debbie said.

"I'm as much a gentleman as you is a cunt."

Spunk winked and Uncle Cousin Debbie shook their head.

Turning back to business, Spunk limped over to a smoking fire pit a few yards from Bory's skid-marked brains. He bent down on one knee and fished out a pile of melted vests. The brown leather was still smoldering as he held them up with a downed tree branch.

"Guess we gotta fashion us some new cuts," he said.

Gary nodded, reaching into the holster on his ankle and bringing out a seven-inch hunting knife. He crossed to Spunk's bike and placed his boot on Borys's neck, while he went to work with the blade, carving up the fly-riddled torso. When he was satisfied with his work, he held up two large flaps of well-shaped flesh.

Spunk looked to Uncle Cousin Debbie. "Don't suppose you have a sewing kit."

"Of course," Debbie said. "You never know when you might need one."

Debbie reached into their bra and pulled out a small plastic case, tossing it to Gary. Spunk used his teeth to tear the MC patches from their burnt cuts and dropped them in Gary's cupped palm. His eyes went to the ground, studying the fresh vest flesh.

"That meat ain't gonna cut it," Spunk said.

"A little snug," Gary conceded. "But it'll fit."

"Naw," Spunk said, looking over at Gary's BSA Lightning where Foxie Bonnie was sprawled out across the seat, taking shallow breaths. "We can't head home till our entire gang's got they cuts."

He gestured to the weeds beside the boathouse.

"Bet ya could get a few nubs off that numb-skull."

"Shaw nuff," Gary said, gazing over his shoulder at Bartek's disembodied head.

***

They were no longer riding twelve strong, but the Filthy Marauders looked as they did before. Their cuts now bore nipples and veins, but their color was swiftly turning brown in the warm morning sun. The fearsome trio caught their first sight of the filthy as they reached the outskirts of Durr City—a caravan of soiled tourists in stained T-shirts and tattered jeans, their bikes and trucks double-parked along the shoulder of the highway, some of them broke down in the middle of the two lane blacktop. Some were passed out on the hoods of their vehicles, others were squatting in the sagebrush, forcing waste out of themselves while toking on too-large spliffs, and all of them looked ready to hurl some toilet bowls and spit some seeds. These were their people. White ones, black ones, yellow ones, red ones. Filthy mothertruckers of every kink and stink known to modern society and all of them convened in one place with one shared purpose—to turn up and embrace their inner demon.

There were fluffy cumulus clouds hanging low in the blue sky above them as they made their way up a steep hill bound for the clubhouse at the other end of the coast. Spunk wondered if it was gonna rain and what that might do to any traces they may have left behind, but it didn't really concern him. Nothing concerned him as the force of the ride blew the flesh of his face back toward his ears and the rumble filled his head. Nothing mattered but the moment and the moment was as perfect as a sea siren with tits full of lobster bisque.

The Filthy Marauders loosened their clutches and coasted down the other side of the hill, howling like a pack of wolves, and pointing their machines in the direction of home.

AUTHOR'S NOTE

The following is a short story entitled Stuffing, which was originally intended for publication in some gross-out horror anthology. Six or seven years later, I cannot really remember what that anthology was called or who was holding an open call for stories to put in it. What I can tell you, however, is that Stuffing never made it into the intended volume. After reading The Dirty Rooster Fuck-Off, you can make of that what you will.

At some point in 2016, I was invited by my friend and former colleague Jake McGee to work on the relaunch of Kotori, a magazine that held and continues to hold a special place in both of our hearts. It was the first long-term writing gig I ever had and, even though it didn't really pay anything, it was the best gig in town. We got to run the show, managing content, working with our publisher and editor-in-chief on each issues' themes, and getting away with murder.

After the original print version of Kotori was published in the early 2000s, my fellow editors would frequently receive hate mail from interview subjects, record labels, and other clowns who were unhappy with how I wrote about them or their product. A punk rock legend, a movie star, and a certain Harvard professor were among this unhappy lot. Not only did our editor-in-chief defend the offensive writing, he continued to gas us up.

When I think about Stuffing, which was finally

published to the newly-relaunched online edition of Kotori some time in 2016, I think about being full, which is exactly what I was when I was writing for Kotori. There was no monthly paycheck , no guarantee of a cash advance, and no promise of being able to pay the rent. But our bellies were always full of fire, and we could get into any event we wanted to, which is exactly what made us whole.

—SHORT STORY—
STUFFING
———

Cooter wuddn't thankful for shit this holiday season. Not even the ordinary stuff like family or homestead.

His home was a room over the stables, with a rickety rooftop that sent a steady dribble of everything from acidic rainwater to acerbic toads rainin' down on his country ass.

And family? Har! Most of his kin hated his guts worse than they did homosexuals or hygiene. All his brothers—Floyd, Duke, Doc, Forrest, Garth and Bodean—showed him no kind of attention save for sticking fingers in his asshole, while his sister, Eunice, held him down in the hog pen.

Even then the only reason they touched him was so they could holler their cruel nursery rhyme. Here comes a Cooter/Cheesy pea-shooter/Stick his snout inside himself/You'll see he smells like tuna/Here comes The Cooter/Shit-pants full o' manure/His mouth taste like a drooper/'Cause he drinks straight from the sewer.

Cooter hated that song almost as much as he hated being the only black kid in an otherwise all-white home for orphans. Every time his hilljack brood were mean he'd shout, "I swear, one o' these days I'ma straight snuff yer asses."

No one believed it. They had the guns. They had the numbers. There were no Gats there, just J.R. with his buck-shot and Nanna with her antique armaments with cobwebbed barrels more backed up'n ole Floyd's corn-shoot after a binding meal.

"I'll get these crackers yet," Cooter told himself as he sobbed into his pillow and pawed at his scabrous anal fissures.

The next morning was Thanksgiving, the day white folk celebrated the anniversary of their raping and pillaging of the country's native sons. As his bastard brethren pictured the cranberry sauce and turkey flambe they had to look forward to at supper, Cooter had fevered visions of his own, first of the Trail of Tears, callused caravan of natives marching to their death, then images of arrowheads and spears bubbling up in their place; he saw himself brandishing a tomahawk and splitting the dome of his youngest foster brother, peeling his scalp back and pissing on his skull, and the others good and well skull-fucked by the fright of it, scurrying for the nearest exit in tears and sheer terror. And him laughing after them, spraying the whole room with venom-tipped arrows from his quiver as he smiled and smoked some strong kush from a peace pipe.

This reverie was rudely interrupted by the accosting musk of Floyd's sweat-drenched pubes as the eldest of the orphans body- slammed young Cooter and trapped Coot's mug in his massive armpit.

"Har! Har! Teach ya to be dreamin' yer clammy dreams while we're s'pposed to be doin' chores," Floyd yapped. "C'mon, Brillo-head. Paw wants you. Now git or he'll tan your nappy hide!"

Cooter scooted off the soggy, yellowed mattress he shared with the studs and scurried across the barnyard to the house. There he found Paw sprawled out in front of the idiot box, empty fifth of Jack Gagger whiskey in his hand and a boll weevil gnawing at his naked gut, a hairy mound of grease with a deep cleft in the center, out of which spilled lint fit for a nest.

Paw was a corpulent slob who used to work for the railroad till he got athlete's foot and started collecting disability. Ever since he drew that welfare check he'd been a slab of immovable meat in that very same seat, a mess of coiled springs and torn fabric that had once resembled a La-Z-Boy. There he sat, a crooked Merkin on under a grime-encrusted trucker hat, eyes glued to that goo tube, rabbit-eared TV he'd shot enough wads at to qualify for world record of gerkin jerkin.

"Hi Paw," Cooter said softly. "H-happy Thanksgiving... I guess."

"Don't hi me, boy! What thanks do I get? Put a roof over y'alls heads and get four hundred measly bucks a month for puttin' food in your ingrate gullets and thass awl I git? Shit on that arrangement, son! This's the last time!"

Cooter's hands curled into fists. He hadn't seen a dime of that money. Not one new shirt, not even after his brothers used the one on his back as a cum rag twelve months running. He was ready to strike Paw in his pregnant drunkard gut when...

Doc, the cross-eyed runt of the litter, scampered in from the kitchen and threw himself into Paw's arms. The force of the child's weight against him knocked the old man's bowels loose on the shag carpet. Luckily, the family dog, a mongrel with one leg and three wonky eyes, ran over to nip at it, fixing himself whatever meal he could make out of the steaming clump.

Doc whispered into Paw's cauliflower ear. A hush fell over the room. All eyes fell on Cooter in muted awe.

"What, maaaan?" Cooter had had enough.

"Nanna wants you." The old bitch in the

kitchen. But why? Cooter wondered.

"You heard me, boy?!" Paw growled.

"Yeah."

"Then git! 'fore you taste my boot!"

Cooter crept into the nook and looked up at the geriatric, her varicose vag lips dragging on the dusty linoleum floor like a gorilla's knuckles, breasts swinging like floppy pendulums. He could smell her senior stink, but also something else, something overwhelming.

"Blackberries?" he asked.

"Sagacious nose," the old crone crowed. "That's why I picked you." Jabbing a pointy skeleton finger in his forehead. "You're sharp. Not like my kin. You're a good boy, that's why you're gonna get to make Thanksgiving supper with me."

"But I wouldn't know how," he said.

"Sure you would," the fossil said, flashing a grizzled grin. "You want them to taste yer shit as much as I do. So let's give 'em what we got, make 'em thankful they got strong stomachs, eh?"

And with that the caustic cook was on.

Cooter handed Nanna a light bulb and she broke it beneath her house slippers. He brushed up the bits and she dumped them in with pits. She jerked him off real proud and he produced a quart on a trowel. She sopped the rest up with her tongue and spit on a ladle and into the meat loaf it went.

Soon all ingredients were in the stew, potatoes mashed with cheesy feet and gravy giblets made from poo, fresh dumplings rolled from both their bowels, each doled out with their own greasy trowel.

With starters done they licked the main course, hoisting the turkey up and slamming it down where Nanna could clamber up on to the counter and scissor herself with the drumsticks, while Cooter plucked dingleberries from his choad and cheered her on.

When all that was done, Nanna worked on the sauce, scooping Sissy's premenstrual snatch pad outta the trash can for cranberry color. Then she encouraged Cooter to select a special ingredient for their dreadful dross.

"It has to be something that means something to you and also to them. Something'll get the goats of your slut sister and bastard brothers."

Cooter nodded, knowing just what to do. He slunk off with a two-pronged fork and returned to the living room.

When Cooter returned, his Nanna was so taken with his selection that she pressed him to her bulbous bosom and they each sprouted an erection. And so it was that Cooter and Nana joined hand in hand and humped the kitchen counter, taking turns at pumping the turkey's neck-hole.

For the pièce de résistance, every year Nanna made her specialty, the Turducken, a de-boned duck inside a de-boned game hen inside a plump Butterball. Only this year the birds wouldn't be free of bones and the butter would not be believed as butter.

Cooter was ugly and unpopular, this much was true. And he was black, which set him back a ways in their parts. But drop some logic on those fools he did that holiday season. As he and Nanna wheeled out their Thanksgiving supper, all stood in dour honor and hunger, heads bowed in admiration for Cooter, the chosen grandson.

After a prayer, they each dug in, ravenous as they buried their slick faces in slimy strips of browned skin and fluffy taters. Those gray curlies made delicious sprouts! And everyone—Floyd, Duke, Doc, Forrest, Garth and Bodean, and lil

Sissy—licked their fingers clean, mming and ooing as they inhaled their plates. Then their mitts fought over scraps, snatching the last of the bird and one made the fatal mistake of asking, "Why's them sausages so thick all knotted up in this here rib cage?"

And as Garth gobbled and swallowed, Cooter hooked his thumb in the air, gesturing to the La-Z-Boy where Paw sat, gutted. And that's when everyone seated at the table puked in a hue brown, green and yellow—brown from the "giblets," green from the globules, and yellow from a mixture of Nanna's piss and Cooter's jizz.

Nanna brought up her cane, waving it in their faces, saying, "Grab yerselves some straws, now, brats! Show the good Lord y'ain't ungrateful!"

AUTHOR'S NOTE

I started writing The Pink Sock in the first months of 2014 after leaving the world of freelance journalism behind. Crime novelist Terrill Lankford once advised me against fiction writing, calling the form a "black hole." What he didn't tell me was that fiction writing of any kind is as much of a hustle as any other kind of freelancing. In my first few years of submitting short stories to anthologies and magazines, I found that there were editors even worse than those in the world of news publishing.

Where freelance journalists can expect to start out making as little as $75 an article without expenses, the fiction novice is lucky to make anything at all. The sheer volume of publishers expecting something for nothing is staggering. The writers themselves are part of the problem; most aspiring authors are so desperate to see their name on something that they'll give it away for free in return for dubious exposure. This devalues their craft and perpetuates the cycle of exploitation.

I have been guilty of this myself, both as an author and as someone in a position to publish the work of others. As an associate editor, I paid contributors in kind words and DVDs. The cycle continues.

At the time that I wrote The Pink Sock, I had tired of submitting my more serious work to "strangers" and decided to write one for a friend.

As it turned out, The Pink Sock would become the first short story I ever had published. It was placed with my old pal Alex S. Johnson's now-shuttered Nocturnicorn Publishing. The "press" was really just Alex compiling anthologies in his living room, but that's part of the charm of indie publishing and, certainly, why so many of us read indie fiction—it possesses a spartan intimacy that you won't get from any of the big houses.

Writing The Pink Sock and having it published for free by a buddy was a lot like writing for Kotori. The pay sucked, but my gut was full of fire, and I was having a blast. The high you get when you see your name on something for the first time is right up there with any other first-time rush, whether it be one that starts between your legs, down a highway, or up your nose. You'll never forget it and you'll never recapture it, but if you call yourself a writer, it's unlikely that you'll ever stop chasing it. Chase it too hard and you might end up broke.

I include The Pink Sock here because I like to think that its universe is one that could exist on the outskirts of The Dirty Rooster Fuck-Off's fictional Delacroix County. After all, Savannah (the story's protagonist) could very easily be a distant relative of Uncle Cousin Debbie's.

Over the years, these stories have fallen out of print, for reasons obvious and not so obvious. Now that they are bundled up with The Filthy Marauders, I feel like they are safely guarded. Enjoy them at your risk.

—SHORT STORY—
THE PINK SOCK

Where Savannah Slurp grew up, every girl wanted to be in porn. The second oldest profession was second only to marrying a Meth cook in terms of the social cache that came with it. The local kids started training early for it, so when most American middle-school boys were making eyes at their first muff from a tenuous perch beneath a cafeteria table, straining their pubescent peepers to get a glimpse of a hairless hair pie through the relative chastity belt of white cotton panties, the horned-up lads at Savannah's junior high were jacking it openly in gym glass to the sight of thirteen-year old sophomore gals sitting spread eagle on the bleachers, each of them sucking and gagging on suggestively-long lollipop sticks.

Savannah came of age just like her girlfriends, giving gobble jobs to the Go-Mart clerks on Friday nights, in exchange for their solemn promise to share camera phone pics of the act with any prospective porn producers that might stop in for a Slushee. And in the summer time, she'd routinely sign herself up for Slut Camp, so as to ensure that she'd return to school the following year with some new tricks in her bang bag.

But while the rest of her graduating class were spirited away to Uh-Uh-Uh University on full analingual scholarships, Savannah was left behind a year when a discerning proctor took note of her nagging inability to swallow his spores. Savannah was swiftly transferred to a TLC (Teaching Love of Cum) class where, upon closer inspection, it became all too apparent to Nina Hartley High faculty that Savannah had failed to complete so much as one of her handjob-rimjob homework assignments during her tenure with the school. What's more, Savannah was unable or, at least, unwilling to complete any forthcoming exams.

The pulling and subsequent tugging of her school records revealed that her advancement from one grade to the next had been the result of several sexually-spent teachers giving her an easy A for Ambition. To wit: Savannah had a nice pair of tits. And she was well-liked by boys her own age. She had a healthy history of dating and of giving age-appropriate brain. In the classroom, she was attentive to demonstrations by her sexual educators and was first in line for proper protection. Despite her very obvious learning deficit, Savannah earned a reputation as a model student based on her salacious smile and hot bod.

This was all taken into consideration when the Board of Education convened for their final quarterly review and determined Savannah's fate. They had vigorously debated said fate for more than an hour of verbal and physical exertion, perspiring like mad and shouting before reaching a climax that seemed to satisfy them all.

Although their first inclination was to leave Savannah back for her second time running, vice principal Shmaltzy Shmedrick took a sentimental tact and declared, "What effect do you think that would have on this girls' self-esteem and sexual prowess when she's towering over girls with shorter legs and less pubic hair and watching them all come and go and coming all over the place? Forget squirting, she'll never learn to swallow in such a psychologically damaging environment."

The rest of the board members heard Shmaltzy out, but they remained skeptical. Fortunately for young Ms. Slurp, Shmaltzy had left her usual bagged lunch (a banana and a protein shake) at home that day and, thus, proceeded to persuade her fellow board members repeatedly with her warm palm and wet mouth. In short, Shmaltz got several ounces of her required daily protein intake and Savannah got to thrust forward into the anal annals of higher academia.

Savannah managed to skate by on looks alone for her first semester in community cuntelage, but it wasn't long nor short, but, rather, wilting and dry before she recognized her own learning curve. In high school a girl could get away with seeming chaste and inexperienced. In fact, there was a segment of the teaching population that encouraged such behavior, such as Mr. Stockwell in Barely Legal 101. Stockwell groomed his girls for life on the battlefield of teen reem tournaments and amateur child porn try-outs, but by and large, there wasn't a single professor in the field of community cuntelage who would tolerate a young lady without a love for being lathered.

After a hard day's night of handing out hand jobs to strap-hangers as Cumtroller for the San Fernando Transportation Authority, Savannah was always bushed. When she would return to her basement apartment in the Fudge-packing District, she would invariably cry herself to sleep or stomach illness while gazing at the report cards rammed through her mail slot by a rapacious deliveryman, every one of them detailing the utter disgust she exhibited for the free-flowing effluvia of the male reproductive organ.

It wasn't that Savannah was a lousy lay in

general or an unappreciative sexual partner. Indeed, when she was still dating, Lil Miss Slurp had tongued her suitors' balls generously and even, on occasion, offered up an index finger for a proper prostate assist. Not once had she ever filed a complaint when a suitor's ravenous shit shoot inevitably swallowed up her all-state varsity cock-sucking ring and refused to spit it back out. No, the only problem with Savannah was a genetic one—she was a natural born spitter; Savannah simply couldn't stand the sight of sperm. Sex itself was, in her eyes, a many splendored thing, up there with fine dining, barbershop music, and badminton (or shuttlecock, if you prefer).

The conundrum was the condom—it sat there after the ugly-bumping act like a cunning snake posing as a docile worm, its insides visible from the outside as a white-hot slop of grimy intent, its rimmed end matched only by its reservoir tip as a sight that inspired suspicion. Furthermore, the contents themselves, those exiled spermatazoa sent off as castaways into the scumbag in question, appeared to Savannah's engorged Anime eyes as alive and iniquitous, a batch of microscopic and evil amoeba awaiting their chance to strike without warning.

It all boiled down to association and Savannah, unconsciously or no, associated semen with amphibious monsters, the corollary of long-suppressed memories from her cruddy youth. See, before middle school, before varsity cock-sucking triathlons and college sperm cocktail scholarships, before Savannah ever worried about growing up to be a big, important porn star, Lil Ms. Slurp's step dad Arlen Axelrod had taken her on a fishing trip while her mother underwent a hysterectomy. And while mama was under the knife, baby girl was trucked off to a dank forest of overgrown bush and sailed off in an oblong, some would say crooked, kayak with Mr. Axelrod, whose interest in fishing was limited only to the smell of that which he intended to catch and trap.

Arlen and Savannah never caught any fish that day, so Arlen, good and righteously blotto off a cooler full of Schlitz, settled for the next best thing—the would-be daughter-in-law he dubbed "my chicken of the sea."

Letting his plaid jumpsuit sag around his knees, Ole Arlen unleashed what he called his "sssnake" on young Savannah, all of eleven years old at the time, and he told her it was time to play catch and release. "Open yer mouth," he instructed. "Catch what my cod has to deliver and I'll release you later so you can have some dinner!"

Before Savannah could protest, Arlen was pulling his pud. He grabbed that pecker with both hands and worked his scaly, flabby foreskin back and forth at breakneck pace, squeezing his two red onion testis till they produced their ripe, rotten, stinking reward. As Lil Ms. Slurp sagged against the back of the kayak, rocking back and forth, the blast caught her in her face and hair and she fell overboard.

To Savannah, getting drizzled in jizzom or chugging throat yogurt would always be equated with getting hosed and drowning. It was, for this simple reason, that she couldn't accept the skeet, that blast of a facial that would forever guarantee her a spot in the much-coveted ranks of porn's crème de la crème.

She kept telling herself, there's gotta be another way in, something else she could do that would get her a career as a starlet without being a cum dumpster. She had all but given up hope when she accidentally stumbled and fell over her secret, innate gift.

In her haste to become a star, Savannah had starved herself to stay skinny, unaware as she was of the niche her natural self could have carved out in the realm of BBW vids. She ate less and less as her college tuition fund ran out until, eventually, she did away with anything that would even remotely qualify as dietary fiber, subsisting instead on Diet Cola and stale hot dog buns alone.

Over time she stopped going to the bathroom except to stick a fist down her throat to induce vomiting after cheating on her diet with a square of chocolate. She hardly noticed that it had been several weeks since she'd taken a shit when, one lonely afternoon, she awoke with unbearable pains in her abdomen. Her stomach was talking too, grumbling at her for depriving it of a meal, and what was weirder was, she believed she could understand what it was saying. Let me go. Get this monster out of me!

Taking her tummy's words seriously, Savannah rushed to the restroom and flopped down on the bowl. She pushed, but nothing came out. She pushed again. Nothing.

She was about to get up and call it a day when an unspeakable sound of anguish issued from her guts, a sound like a pussy fart amplified by subwoofers. She listened to its cry as if it were a viking god she must obey, a god that had given her a power she didn't know she had, but which she would do anything to retain.

Gathering all the strength she could muster, and grabbing hold of the towel rod and the sink top for ballast, Savannah clamped her fingers into fists, squeezed her eyes shut and willed blood, sweat and tears from her pretty pink pores, all in the name of

loosing whatever horrible lecherous beast was dwelling inside. Puffy pillow lips pursed, she was determined.
Push.
Nothing.
Puuuuush!
Nada.
GRRRRRRRRRR!!!
Aaaaaaand...
...!pink!...
It wasn't the color pink, pink was the sound, the little bing one would expect from an uncooked pea landing on a tin roof, the noise a needle point might make if gently dropped on a baking sheet. It was, in short, a turd that hardly deserved to carry its name, so small and insignificant was its diminutive creamy-brown circumference.

"That's the monster?" Savannah said to herself. "That's what was making that big ruckus?" Wiping the perspiration from her chiseled but pimply cheeks, she shook her head and sighed, then let out a laugh that was substantially louder than her excretion. "To think you go around worryin' about cruddy, cummy creatures all these years and, in the end, that's what they measure up to. I'll never be afraid again."

But afraid again she was, pud-whacker! Afraid only moments later was she, because as soon as Savannah put weight on her pretty pink soles and went to unbend her knees, her spine was seized by a fresh pain and her inner thighs trembled in a way that was wholly foreign to her.

Writing it off as after effects, a reverberation or phantom thing, Savannah's slender fingers reached for her underwear where they were balled up around her ankles. Leaning forward she chanced a look between her legs, a tentative glance, and that's when she saw it. That's when she came face to face with her gift.

There, in all its flowering and fetid glory, was her intestine, running rich with hues of purple and blue, and painted in a psychedelic latticework of lovely, robust capillaries. It bulged from between her dimpled butt cheeks, a bulbous bulb of pure purple-and-pink awesomeness, glistening and supple, shining under the light penetrating the windowpane over the toilet.

After mastering her new craft, after it seemed that she had worked out all the kinks and learned how to control it, Savannah took her special gift to town. In no time at all she had managed to use her high school bestie as a reference and book herself a gig appearing in Ronny "The Wrench" Remington's new fetish DVD for coprophiles.

When she showed up at the set, a mansion somewhere deep in the San Fernando Valley mountains, Savannah was hot to trot and ready to get stuck right and proper. Moxie oozed off her porcelain skin like steam-heat off an active kettle. Her first scene, double-teaming a pair of midgets named Fuckface and Shithead, went off as a smashing success, with her grinning coquettishly for the camera, while sitting on their faces and grinding. The sequence ended with the two internalizing their orgasms, a new trend in Tantric Porn, in anticipation of the following session.

The dandy randy dwarves hosed themselves off and massaged their manhoods delicately with Novocaine to withhold any premature spurts, while Savannah retired to her new dressing room to beam at herself in the mirror. This was it! Her big moment! She could hardly believe it herself.

With a celebratory swig off a champagne flute and a bird-size nibble of some Crunchy Taco

Hamburger Helper, Savannah winked at herself in the mirror and strutted out to make cinematic history.

On her way she practiced her anal exercises, clenching and unclenching her butt muscles. Her muscles relaxed as she reached the lime green shag carpet where lights and screens had been erected and her co-stars waited on a futon beneath an array of strobes and a boom mic. Once there, Savannah dropped trou and she smiled in good humor at the Lilliputians poised on the fuck-ready furniture.

But the smile faded quick when she saw the two dwarves get sick and spew lime green sputum on each others' chins. Then the camera man hurled and the director did a spit take and the boom girl tossed her cookies and the script girl slipped in the puke and cracked her head open, spewing blood in the vomitus and, as the floor around her ankles was flooded in bile and spit, Savannah looked down and saw that she'd totally blown it.

Where once was a flowering puckered little thing, a firm, glistening specimen deserving of a nibble or nip, there was a swollen monstrosity filled to its brim with her shit. You could see the fecal matter through it dermis of purple-blue film just the way that she'd looked through a condom at what was within. And there it dangled, getting larger and expanding, like the bitterness built up inside after years of yearning—a prolapsed organ attached to others and spilling out until there was nothing left... until Savannah's desire had turned her inside out.

Savannah Slurp was gone in a spurt, but what remained was a mystery. Soon they'd have names for it, slang and fame for it. Soon there'd be a brand-spanking new trend.

Yea, soon there were guys who couldn't get hard

unless they watched them some Kerplunkage. Soon there were dudes whose dicks would just droop unless they inhaled the Scratch-N-Sniff clamshell box to Curdled In A Girdle Vol. III: Organ Porkers. Soon the phrase "GRRRLORPSH!!" became a world-famous texters' exclamation and the actual sound of it put lead in people's pencils.

To say Savannah Slurp pioneered a genre is like saying Jesus was one helluva guy. Savannah Slurp was immortalized as more than just a porn star. Savannah Slurp went down as the one chick who ever became a desire personified.

She didn't dig fluids, she became a fluid. She didn't get famous chugging things from orifices, she became the orifice. You ask anyone today and they'll tell you, sex is always a lot stranger and a lot more satisfying if you turn your socks inside out.

ABOUT THE AUTHOR

Bob Freville is the author of *Battering the Stem* and *The Network People*. More recently, his satirical mystery *The Proud and the Dumb* landed on the Godless bestseller list.

Freville's work has been published by Akashic Books, Creem, Horror Sleaze Trash, Kush, and more.

Sign up and subscribe to his newsletter at:
https://moderncustodian.substack.com/

NOVELS FROM
THE EVIL COOKIE PUBLISHING

ANTHOLOGIES FROM THE EVIL COOKIE PUBLISHING

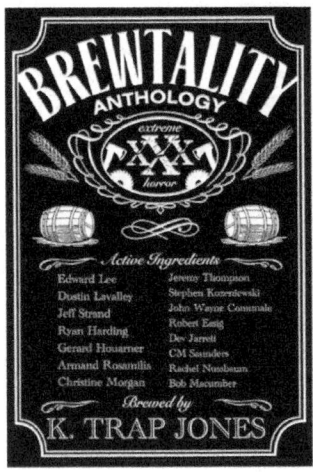

www.theevilcookie.com